1

Billie Haney suppressed a yawn and reached for his coffee mug.

"You'll get used to it," Frank Carlson said, smiling at his young co-worker. "After a month on the graveyard shift, you'll never want to work days again."

"Yeah, right," Haney answered as he rolled his shoulders. He hoped he never got the chance to get used to this job. Working midnight to eight, checking cars and trucks in through a gate, wasn't his idea of a career. He was only going to collect a few paychecks, then find a real job. Maybe he would move to Des Moines or even Chicago. There was nothing to hold him anymore in Ames, Iowa.

His parents were talking about closing the family hardware store and moving to Florida. They couldn't compete with the new K-Mart out on U.S. 30. Business was so bad that they hadn't even been able to hire their own son. Most of his friends from high school had either gone away to college or packed up and headed for the big city lights. For guys his age the only other jobs available, besides the minimum-wage rent-a-cop position, were busing tables or pumping gas.

Frank Carlson, his face heavily lined and the color of oiled leather, shook his head as he poured himself another cup of strong coffee. For twelve years Carlson had worked forty hours a week as a security guard for BioTech, Inc. His income made the difference between keeping the farm that had been in the family for six generations or losing it to the bank. He knew how Billie felt; he had left town when he was the same age. But the roots were too deep. When his father died, he had returned home and taken over the farm, debt and all. Although it had meant he'd had to take on another job, he was determined the land would stay in the Carlson family.

"What the...?" Billie Haney began, pointing at something heading up the driveway toward the main gate.

Carlson put his cup down and strained to see what was moving in the predawn gloom. Just beyond the point where the lights of the plant fully lit the area, a toy tank, about three feet long and eighteen inches high, was moving across the pavement in their direction. The radio-controlled device appeared to be an exact scale model of the new M-1 tank.

Haney reached for his gun, but Carlson stopped him. "It's probably one of George's practical jokes." George Winston worked the four-to-midnight shift. To break the tedium of the job, he would set a trap for Carlson at least once a week. Sometimes he would tamper with the coffee. Other times he would move the balance weights on the security barricade that blocked the entrance, making it impossible to lift. This stunt had George's name written all over it.

Carlson strained his eyes in an effort to see where George was hiding. He knew that if he charged out of the guard station with gun in hand, he would never hear the end of it. He decided to play it cool and remain in the boxy six-by-six building.

"That's really neat," Haney said as he peered through the glass.

"I can't wait to see what it'll do next," Carlson said.

The toy tank scooted under the reinforced lift gate that crossed the main entrance to the plant and pulled up beside the guard station.

"Hell," Carlson said. "Let George have his fun. I want to get a look at this thing."

HERBERT QUEENSBURY'S breath came in short gulps as he watched the tank pull up to the guard station. His eyes gleamed. His lips were moist. "That's it, that's it," he said to the man next to him on the passenger seat of the van. The other four men sat silently in the rear, watching the two men in the front.

The tank was controlled by the seven-channel transmitter in Kevin Pitts's lap. The thin young man had helped Queensbury design the system. "This is fun," Pitts said. "Wait till they're hit with the knockout gas."

Herbert Queensbury licked his lips. "Yes, won't they be surprised." Now forty-six, Queensbury had been bald since his mid-thirties. At five-five and weighing in at slightly over two hundred pounds, he wasn't a great physical specimen. The only impressive thing about him was his IQ; it was higher than his weight.

The six men in the van watched as the tank moved into position. The smallest of the four sitting in the back was still well over six feet tall, and none weighed less than 220. They looked like the kind of guys you would want on your side in a barroom brawl.

Pitts wrinkled his forehead till his eyebrows touched in the middle. "She sure is moving slow tonight." Kevin Pitts had spent hours in his backyard mastering the controls of the tank. "I've never seen it quite this sluggish before."

"Must be the added weight," Queensbury said.

"Oh, that's right, the knockout gas."

"Yes, the gas." Queensbury pressed a finger to his lips to hold back his smile. "I believe it's close enough now."

Pitts nodded his agreement. He slipped a key into the control box, and an amber light immediately flashed. "It's armed." Pitts looked longingly at the red button at the center of the control box. "Can I, I mean, ah . . ." he stammered.

"Of course," Queensbury answered. "Without you I would never have discovered what BioTech was making here. You've earned the right to help put an end to this horror."

Kevin Pitts's chest swelled with pride at the compliment. When he had graduated from Cal Tech, he had wanted to aid mankind, and tonight he was taking a big step toward that goal. He had gone to work for BioTech with the hope of discovering a new, nonpolluting fertilizer. Instead, he had ended up in Ames making weapons for the military. The day he had discovered Queensbury through a computer billboard, his world had changed. He knew he would lose his job for what he was about to do, but that didn't matter. He had already accepted a position with another biological engineering firm in Sunnyvale, California. The new job wasn't perfect, but at least he wouldn't be working for the Pentagon any longer.

Tonight's mission was simple: once they'd penetrated security they would steal a quantity of the toxin produced at the plant. Then they would present it to Greenpeace, which would go public with the Pentagon's secret. Congress and the press would close the project down.

Pitts placed his finger on the button. "Here goes nothing."

"Considerably more than nothing, Kevin," Queensbury said.

Kevin Pitts hesitated for a moment, then glanced at Queensbury for the final approval. Queensbury granted permission with a nod. The young man pushed the button.

The instant the button was depressed, a blinding fireball erupted and the guard's station was reduced to smoldering kindling. From their distant position the light of the explosion arrived half a second before the sound. The shock waves shook the van.

Kevin Pitts dropped the control box and turned in horror toward Queensbury. "My God, what happened?"

An evil smile twisted the corners of Herbert Queensbury's mouth. "I would say you just killed two people."

"Me!" The young man's eyes were filled with terror and confusion. "I don't understand, Mr. Queensbury."

"Please, all of my friends call me the Gamesmaster."

Kevin Pitts's eyes grew large. He had heard the name before, always spoken in connection with an act of terrorism. Pitts reached for the handle of the door, but a spring-loaded, lead-filled sap came crashing down on the back of his head.

"Don't kill him," the Gamesmaster said softly. "We still need him. And now we must proceed."

By the time they reached the main entrance, one of Queensbury's men had pulled Kevin Pitts to the rear of the van and trussed him up like a calf ready for branding. A handkerchief was shoved into his mouth and several strips of white tape were placed over it.

The force of the explosion had not only leveled the guard station, it had blown open the main gate. The six-inch steel pole that normally blocked the entrance had skewered a pickup truck in the parking lot a full ten yards from the entrance. Queensbury had to swerve to the left to avoid the crater the exploding tank had left in the pavement.

"Gentlemen," Queensbury shouted over his shoulder, "I need not remind you that we must be in and out quickly." He knew that, although miles from town, someone would have seen or heard the explosion.

Each of the four men had an AK-47 lying across his lap and a half-dozen hand grenades attached to his belt. Queensbury followed the map Pitts had drawn to a low white building with a red number three painted on the side. Before he could back the van into the side loading dock, one of the twelve overhead doors in the cargo loading area began to go up. A custodian, hearing the noise, had come to investigate.

One of the men kicked the rear door of the van open and fed a round into the hungry AK-47.

"Hey, what's going on out here?" the janitor shouted. His answer came from the mouth of the Soviet-made assault rifle. Three 7.62 mm rounds thundered out at 2,330 feet per second and slammed into the startled man's chest. The first bullet pushed

the custodian backward, the second and third spun
him to the ground. The holes in his chest made a
gurgling, hissing sound as he drew in his last breath.

"Let's go!" Queensbury shouted as he checked his
watch.

The five men charged through the doorway toward their target in the rear of the warehouse. The
door to the security area was steel and at least three
inches thick. Queensbury pressed plastic explosives
next to the doorknob and behind each of the three
hinges. He inserted detonators into the mounds as
the others looked for cover. Finally Queensbury
joined his men behind a row of wooden crates ten
yards from the door. When his finger touched the
button on the remote control unit, the heavy door
toppled forward and hit the concrete floor with a
thud.

The blast triggered the security system. A loud bell
began to clang. A siren on the roof of the building
began to howl. The five men charged in through the
smoke and haze. The light switch to the room had
been blown away with the door; the raiders had to
use their flashlights.

"There," Queensbury shouted as he pointed at
two sets of shelves. Each shelf held twelve one-gallon
glass bottles encased in two inches of impact-resistant
plastic. On one set of shelves the bottles were bright
yellow, on the other pitch-black. The bottles could
be dropped off a three-story building without
breaking. The warning labels on the bottles gave no

clue about their contents except to àdvise that they be handled with care.

"How many, Gamesmaster?" one of the men asked in a dull monotone.

"Eight of each. Now hurry."

Two of the men slung their AK-47s over their shoulders and began placing the bottles in a strong plastic box. The box had twenty-four slots, was lined with sponge foam and had been custom-built to hold their prize.

"There's room for a dozen of each, Gamesmaster."

Queensbury checked his watch. "No, we need to leave *now*."

The two men finished placing the bottles in the container and, grabbing opposite ends of the box, began to sprint toward the outside door. They secured the box in the rear of the paneled van, and all five were about to climb aboard when they heard the fast-approaching sound of a siren. The police car would arrive in a matter of moments.

"We'll deal with the police on the way out."

Kevin Pitts had regained consciousness. At the first glimpse of the special container used only for the black and yellow bottles, he began to scream into his gag. His eyes were wide with terror. The young man began to struggle against his bonds but to no avail. The leader of the four toughs, a man named Sonny Hayes, roughly shoved Pitts away from the weapons crate he was leaning against. Pitts continued to kick and squirm until the butt of an AK-47, delivered to the back of his head, sent him back to dreamland.

Sonny's brother, B.J., dropped his AK-47, opened the crate and pulled out a Pancor Jackhammer. The 12-gauge shotgun had a ten-round rotary magazine located behind the trigger. Able to fire at full automatic, the Jackhammer was a fearsome piece of hardware.

The van inched away from the loading dock just as the police car rounded the corner. Queensbury floored the gas and flew by the car in the opposite direction. The cop slammed on his brakes and cut the wheel hard. The car did a tight 180-degree turn and was immediately in hot pursuit.

The police car, a Dodge with a big V-8 and a heavy suspension, quickly closed the gap and was less than twenty yards behind the van by the time they reached the main gate. Queensbury refused to slow down, and the van was jolted and shaken by the debris in the road as they passed the smoldering guard station.

Checking his rearview mirror, Queensbury let up a bit on the gas and allowed the police car to pull within ten feet. "Now!" he shouted.

Sonny kicked the rear door open, then dived for cover. The other three, including B.J. with his Pancor Jackhammer, opened fire.

The 7.62 rounds from the AK-47 peppered the police car, but the Pancor did the real damage. The first three blasts from the Jackhammer took out the windshield and the radiator of the vehicle. Number four hit the policeman just below the left eye, turning the interior of the car bright red. It veered to the left; the headless driver was no longer steering, but his foot was still frozen to the gas pedal.

The car plowed into a culvert near the side of the road, and as it came up the other side of the ditch, it became airborne. As if in slow motion, the police car rolled over in midair and landed a hundred yards from the highway. Sliding across the ground on its roof, the car sideswiped a tree. The vehicle finally slowed to a stop but continued to rock up and down like a macabre teeter-totter.

"Excellent," Queensberry said. "We should have at least fifteen minutes to make our escape."

Five minutes from the BioTech facility, Queensbury turned off his light and pulled off the road into a stand of trees. Two cars were hidden there: a station wagon and a late-model Ford sedan.

The weapons crate was placed in the trunk of the sedan. One of the men folded down the rear seat of the station wagon and placed the bottles, and then Kevin Pitts, in the back. He flipped a tarp over both.

"You know what to do?" The men all nodded their heads. "Good. Any questions?"

"I have one, Gamesmaster," Sonny Hayes said.

"You've earned it, number one. What?"

"What's in the bottles?"

Herbert Queensbury, the Gamesmaster, smiled a wicked, satisfied smile. "The bottles contain revenge."

The four men looked puzzled. One finally asked, "Revenge against who?"

"Carl Lyons."

2

Carl Lyons pressed his back against a mature elm tree and struggled to control his breathing. The crisp December air had a cold bite, but perspiration had still darkened the front of his shirt and was now starting to sting his eyes. Despite his best efforts, the men stalking him were only minutes behind. Drawing in several deep breaths, he forced much-needed oxygen into his protesting lungs. He checked his watch. He had to hold out for twenty more minutes.

Lyons surveyed the terrain; his options were limited. He could either move south across an open field or continue up the hillside and use the widely spaced trees as cover. The field had patches of weeds, some several feet high, that had survived several hard frosts and hadn't been beaten down by the first snowfall of the season. The trees, even without their leaves, offered the better of the two options.

Carl "Ironman" Lyons, a member of the President's covert-action squad, Able Team, knew they would expect him to stay in the woods, so he opted for the field. Lyons crouched and ran, offering only a low profile to any sniper, before diving into a stand of two-foot high weeds. If they hadn't seen him bolt from the trees, he might have a chance.

Ironman crawled deeper into the undergrowth. He moved slowly with frequent stops, keeping the movement of the weeds minimal in an effort to avoid revealing his position. He resisted the urge to pop his head up and check the location of the team pursuing him; it would be all over if he did.

The winter sun was far enough to the south, and it was late enough in the day so that Lyons was able to find areas of deep shadows among the weeds. With no trees or large rocks for cover, he could only hope that would be enough. Twenty yards to the north two startled quails fluttered from the undergrowth. Lyons didn't move. He didn't even breathe.

"Give it up!" a voice shouted from behind him.

"We've got you!" yelled another man who was only a few yards in front of his position. "We've got you bracketed."

Carl Lyons couldn't argue. He might be trapped, but he wasn't finished. With a bloodcurdling scream he leaped to his feet, weapon drawn, and ran toward the closest voice. Before he could find a target they had located him. The stalkers' guns gently coughed. Lyons felt the impacts, and the front and rear of his shirt erupted in bright crimson.

Ironman had lost.

Fortunately the pellets that had struck him were filled with paint. And the men firing were friends, not enemies. The adult game of hide-and-seek, played with air guns on the back section of Stony Man Farm in Virginia, was over.

"Damn," he said. He dropped his weapon and held up his hands. "I only needed to hold out for ten more minutes and I'd have won."

"Naw," Hermann "Gadgets" Schwarz said as he flipped Lyons a towel to wipe the excess paint off of his shirt. "We could have taken you almost any-time. We just wanted to test the system."

Gadgets looked like something out of a low-budget science fiction movie. His head was covered with an odd-looking device that resembled a motorcycle helmet with a pair of binoculars welded to the front. Pulling the contraption off, he revealed brown hair matted to his scalp.

John "Cowboy" Kissinger, wearing the same headgear, joined the conversation. "It worked great, Carl." Kissinger pulled his unit off and handed it to Lyons. "Take a peek."

Reluctantly Lyons pulled the device over his head. When his eyes adjusted to the sudden change in light, the world turned varying shades of amber. Ironman shrugged his shoulders; it was like using a heavy pair of sunglasses. "What's the big deal?"

"Look down," Gadgets said with a laugh.

Lyons glanced at his feet and did a double take. He could see every step he and the other two men had taken. The footprints were faint red. Retracing his steps, Ironman came to the place where he had crawled through the field. It looked like a wide red stripe. The places where he had stopped were a brighter red.

Lyons pulled off the infrared optical unit that Cowboy and Gadgets had used to track him and looked down again. Nothing. "Pretty neat, but awfully bulky."

"It's new technology," Gadgets answered. "The size and weight will decrease pretty quickly."

"Where did you guys get these things, anyway?"

Gadgets and Cowboy exchanged silly grins. "It's better that you don't know," Cowboy said.

"Accessory after the fact?" Ironman asked.

"Something like that," Gadgets said.

"You're right. I don't want to know. Let's get back to base camp."

Gadgets slapped Cowboy and the two men led the way south. The two had been inseparable since the fancy headgear had arrived. They had spent the morning squirreled away in the workshop where Cowboy performed his magic on the weapons used by the men of Stony Man. Kissinger was the compound's resident gunsmith.

Gadgets had earned his nickname by his uncanny ability to make silk purses out of sows' ears. An electronic whiz, Schwarz had designed and built many of the devices Able Team took for granted.

The three continued south. On the far side of a hill they found the Jeep Gadgets and Cowboy had used.

Lyons, the loser, had to ride on the kidney-busting rear seat while the winners sat up front, gloating.

Lyons had been too confident of his skills. He had figured there was no way the two of them, especially with a fifteen-minute head start, could catch him within the three-hour time allotment. He had been wrong. Lyons had been so sure of himself that he had even allowed Cowboy and Gadgets the use of the Jeep as well as the fancy hats.

Lyons now knew how the ancient samurai must have felt when they had first encountered rifles and cannons. A lifetime of training and discipline was made obsolete in the blink of an eye by a new generation of weapons. Courage and skill with a sword had provided little protection from grapeshot and musket balls. Lyons worried that his skills, the skill of the modern warrior, would someday be replaced by microchips and push buttons. Till then he would just nut up and do it.

They were nearing the unobtrusive set of buildings that made up the Stony Man Farm complex when Gadgets slowed the Jeep to a stop. "What do you make of that, Ironman?"

Lyons squinted into the sun, using his hand to shield his eyes. Coming directly at them was a radio-controlled airplane, one of the largest he had ever seen. The plane had a wingspan of over seven feet.

Lyons, the laconic strategist of Able Team, took charge. "Hit the dirt!" The airplane, despite its harmless appearance, would be treated as a threat till proven otherwise. The three men dived from the Jeep: Gadgets to the left, Cowboy to the right and Lyons out the back.

The plane swooped down, zeroing in on Ironman. Lyons flattened himself on the ground to avoid being hit. Rolling over, he fired a paint pellet as the plane flew by. He wasn't sure if the paint would have any effect, but it was the only weapon he had. Unfortunately the air gun didn't have the muzzle velocity of his trusty Colt Python; the plane was too fast and the pellet was too slow.

The model airplane ignored Gadgets and Cowboy. Whoever was controlling the plane was playing a cat-and-mouse game with Lyons. The gasoline-powered airplane did a tight loop over a stand of trees and headed toward Ironman again.

"Look out!" Kissinger yelled as the model zeroed in on its target.

Lyons rolled hard to the right as the plane buzzed to within a few inches of the ground, just missing him for the second time. After the model flew by, Ironman jumped to his feet and sprinted toward a large oak tree. The plane banked for another pass.

"I've had about enough of this," Lyons said. He motioned for the plane to come at him. "Come and get me!"

The model plane headed straight for Lyons. When it was only inches from his face, Ironman leaned to the left and his right hand shot up like a cobra. He managed to hit the plane as it flew by. With a tearing sound, the paper-and-balsa-wood right wing tore off in his hand.

The plane nose-dived into the ground and spun around in a small circle, kicking up a cloud of dust. Lyons ran over and kicked the crippled plane until the motor had had enough and stopped running.

The three men circled the model. Gadgets squatted on his haunches and studied the wreckage.

"What do you make of it, Gadgets?" Kissinger asked.

"Just an expensive kit, the kind you can buy at any good hobby store or by mail order." Gadgets picked up the main body of the model airplane and stood up. "What I want to know is what it's doing here. And why."

Lyons was fuming. "I have a good idea who's behind this. Let's get back to base camp."

BEFORE THE JEEP had come to a complete stop, Lyons had rolled out of the back and was looking for Rosario Blancanales. Ironman had been suspicious when Blancanales, known as Pol, short for Politician, had passed on joining the manhunt. He obviously had a bad cold, but it was out of character for him to miss the opportunity to embarrass Lyons.

"Where is he?" Lyons roared.

"Who?" Kissinger asked as he flipped the keys to the Jeep to one of the men from the motor pool.

"Pol. Or should I say, Pilot."

"Oh, you think Pol was the one who buzzed you with the airplane." Kissinger had to admit it made sense. Blancanales was famous for his offbeat sense of humor. "There he is," Kissinger said, pointing toward the doorway leading to Aaron "Bear" Kurtzman's computer control center.

Lyons turned on his heels and sprinted toward Blancanales. "Hey," he shouted, "I want a word with you."

"Looks like you lost, Ironman," Pol said as he wiped a handkerchief under his nose.

"You think you're pretty cute, don't you?" Lyons said as he jammed a finger into Pol's chest.

"What?" Pol answered indignantly as he pushed Lyons's hand away. "You're covered with red paint and you're back before the deadline. Sure sounds like you lost to me."

"You know what I'm talking about," Lyons said as he went nose to nose with Blancanales.

"Back off, Ironman."

If it came to blows, it would be an even match. Lyons had the size and the strength. Blancanales, a Black Beret in Vietnam, had the speed to nullify any physical disadvantage. Both men were students of the martial arts.

"You think you're pretty cute," Lyons snarled again as he bumped Pol with his chest. "I ought to tear your head off."

Blancanales held his ground. His eyes were like black stones. He didn't want to fight with Ironman, but they were fast approaching the point of no return. "I don't know what your problem is, Ironman, but you better back off."

Kissinger pulled Lyons back a few steps. "Come on, Ironman. You don't know if it was Pol for sure."

The two friends of many battles glared at each other.

"Did you send out the airplane?" Kissinger questioned.

"What airplane?" Pol asked, never taking his eyes off Ironman.

"The radio-controlled airplane that buzzed us on our way back to base."

"You guys been smokin' those funny cigarettes?"

Kissinger pointed toward Schwarz, who was sitting cross-legged on the ground disassembling the model airplane.

"Hey," Pol said, raising his hands in surrender, his mood softening. "I don't know anything about that. I've been with Bear."

"He's right," said Kurtzman, the wheelchair-bound computer genius of Stony Man. Having heard the ruckus at his front door, he had come to investigate. "He's been with me for the past hour."

"If Pol didn't send the airplane after us," Kissinger asked, "then who did?"

"Maybe this is the answer."

All heads turned toward Gadgets, who had just finished his dissection of the airplane. He had an envelope in his hand. "It's a letter, Ironman. Addressed to you."

3

Carl Lyons tore open the envelope and read the letter inside. His shoulders slumped as his eyes scanned the note for the second time. "I don't believe this."

"What?" the men watching Lyons shouted in four-part harmony. Lyons handed the note to Gadgets, who read it out loud.

> Dear Carl,
> Long time, no see. I'm back on the outside again and would like a rematch. To add excitement to our little game, I've stolen a toxin capable of killing everyone from Washington to Boston. You have forty-eight hours to find me.
>
> Sincerely,
> Herbert Queensbury, the Gamesmaster
>
> P.S. Bring your friends along.

Attached to the note was the label from one of the containers of toxin. Gadgets passed the piece of paper back to Ironman, who studied it in disbelief. "I thought I'd never hear that name again."

"Who is?" Pol asked, checking the note for the name at the bottom. "Who's Herbert Queensbury?"

"I arrested him when I worked for the Justice Department," Lyons said. "I can't believe he's back on the streets."

"What's this thing?" Pol asked as he looked at the torn label attached to the note. Lyons shook his head and shrugged.

"Let me have a look," Kurtzman suggested. The moment the note landed in his lap, a soft whistle escaped his lips.

"You recognize it?" Ironman asked.

"Oh, yeah," Bear answered, shaking his head. "It's from a company named BioTech. They make biological weapons. This stuff was stolen two days ago and everyone in the country is looking for it. In fact, that's why Brognola rounded all of you guys up and called you here."

"What was stolen?" Gadgets asked.

"Like the note says, enough toxin to kill everyone on the eastern seaboard. Would this Queensbury guy use it?" Bear asked grimly.

Lyons didn't hesitate. "Yes."

Kurtzman began wheeling himself back into his electronic cave. "I've got to get hold of Brognola."

"Where," Pol asked, scratching his head, "are we supposed to find this Queensbury guy?"

"He has to be nearby," Gadgets answered.

"Why?"

"The model airplane's radio control has a limited range."

"And," Lyons said, his eyes filling with rage, "he had to be close enough to see us."

"Right," Gadgets agreed.

"What's the airplane's maximum range, Gadgets?" Pol asked.

"In these hills, not more than a mile or two."

"So," Lyons said as he plotted the next move, "he's only a few miles away. Where's Grimaldi?"

"Jack flew Brognola up to Washington about an hour ago," Gadgets told him.

"Is there another chopper pilot available?"

"Wouldn't matter. There are no helicopters here."

Lyons drove his fist into his hand. "Damn. We have an expanding perimeter and no idea in which direction to look." He thought for a moment and then yelled in Kurtzman's direction. "Bear, check with the guards and see if they've seen anything. Anything at all."

"Right," Kurtzman answered from the doorway.

The perimeter of the property that made up Stony Man Farm was patrolled night and day by a highly skilled group of pros. The men who called the secret base home—Able Team, Phoenix Force and the driving engine, Mack Bolan—had many enemies. It had been an earlier attack on Stony Man that had sentenced Aaron Kurtzman to life in a wheelchair.

"Gadgets, what's the range on those fancy glasses of yours?" Lyons asked.

"Unknown."

"Whoever was controlling the airplane had to be west of us."

"Why?"

"He had to have a clear sight line. There was a hill to the east of us, and the north-south valley would have been obstructed by trees. He had to be near the top of one of the hills west of here."

Gadgets nodded. As usual, Ironman's analysis was right on. His mind ran smoother than any of Bear's computers when it came to sizing up a situation.

"Cowboy," Lyons ordered, "get us some real weapons and a couple of Jeeps."

"Right." Kissinger was instantly at a full gallop in the direction of his workshop, shouting directions to the motor pool on the way by.

Pol dashed out of the communications center and rejoined the other men of Able Team. "One of the eastern perimeter guards fails to report."

"You mean western?" Gadgets asked.

"No," Pol answered, a puzzled look on his face. "Eastern."

"There goes your theory, Ironman."

Lyons slowly shook his head. "No, that confirms it. He's to the west."

Two Jeeps squealed up next to the men at about the same time Cowboy arrived with weapons. He hadn't had time to pick and choose; every man got an M-16/M-203 combo. The battle-tested workhorse, after a few hours on Cowboy's workbench, was the backbone of the Able Team arsenal.

"Cowboy," Lyons barked, "you ride with me. Pol, you take Gadgets in the other Jeep."

As soon as Gadgets and Cowboy pulled their strange headgear on, it was clear to Pol why he and Lyons were driving. Hopefully the fancy piece of technology would help to locate their target.

Cowboy was barely in the Jeep when Ironman slammed it into gear and floored the gas. The open-topped four-wheel-drive vehicle roared out of the compound amid a hail of dust and gravel. Pol and Gadgets were only a few yards behind.

The two Jeeps followed a rutted trail east until it ended at a creek bed where water trickled through the smooth stones. Getting across would be a problem. During the rainy season the creek roared with the runoff of the nearby hills. Centuries of rain, snow and sudden thaws had gouged a four-feet-deep barrier. Lyons motioned for Pol to go to the right while he headed left. The two Jeeps headed in opposite directions, seeking a place to cross.

"Slow down, Ironman," Kissinger shouted. "I think I see something."

Lyons slammed on the brakes so hard that the Jeep fishtailed as it jerked to a halt. The sudden stop allowed the dust to catch up and settle on them. "Where?"

"At one o'clock."

Lyons reached under the seat, found a pair of binoculars and scanned the far hillside without any luck. "Where?"

"You got the hill?"

"Yeah."

"Halfway up and ten degrees to the right."

Lyons saw it. A red Bronco 4x4 was nearly hidden behind a stand of trees. Two men, too far away for Lyons to tell if one was Queensbury, were loading equipment into the rear of the truck.

Before Cowboy could reach for his communicator, he heard the scratchy sound of Gadgets's voice. "We've spotted them."

Cowboy pushed the button on the black box attached to his wrist. "Red Bronco, four-tenths of a mile."

"Roger."

"Have you found a spot to cross yet?"

"Negative. Wait, looks like they're leaving."

Lyons had drawn the same conclusions. He slammed the Jeep into reverse, floored the gas and cut the wheel. The vehicle did a tight one-eighty, and they headed back in the direction they'd come from.

"You're not planning on doing what I think you're planning on doing, are you?" Kissinger asked warily.

Lyons didn't answer. His teeth were clenched tight, the muscles in his jaws flexed.

A quarter of a mile back the creek bed narrowed to around ten feet and the bank on the east side was several feet higher than the one on the west. Cowboy knew what Ironman had in mind as he reached for his seat belt.

Lyons swung the Jeep wide to give them enough room to get up to speed. The Jeep began to buck like a green horse as the needle on the speedometer moved higher.

Forty.

Forty-five.

Fifty.

The creek was only a hundred yards away.

Fifty-five.

Cowboy placed his arms in front of his face.

The Jeep was airborne, the four tires spinning like pinwheels. It hit the ground nose first, bounced but didn't flip over. Lyons wrestled with the steering wheel until he regained control. Cowboy glanced over his shoulder; the Jeep had cleared the creek with ten feet to spare.

The Jeep bounced across the meadow, following the dusty rooster tail of the Red Bronco. The powerful Ford had nearly a mile lead and had the additional advantage of driving on a gravel road. Still, Lyons, heading cross-country, was closing the gap.

The Bronco was off the hill and had turned onto a narrow paved lane that headed west toward a notch in the Blue Ridge Mountains. Lyons knew the road: it led to Shenandoah National Park. He pulled up onto the pavement and floored the gas again, closing on the Bronco. The powerful Ford was only doing about forty now.

"I don't like this," Ironman said as the Jeep continued to gain ground.

"What?"

"It's too easy."

In less than a mile the Jeep was abreast of the Bronco. Two teenage boys were the only passengers. Cowboy motioned for the Ford to pull over, but the young driver gave him a one-finger salute as he increased his speed.

"I've had about enough of this," Lyons said, driving with one hand and reaching for his M-16 with the other.

"You just keep us on the road," Cowboy ordered. "I'll get 'em to pull over." When the Jeep was abreast of the Bronco again, Cowboy fired a 3-round burst into the air, then aimed his weapon at the driver. The teenager's eyes widened with fear as the Ford rolled to a stop on the right shoulder.

"Hey, man, what's your problem?" the driver shouted as he stepped from the Bronco. "You some kind of cop or somethin'?"

Lyons spun the kid around and patted him down. He was clean. Cowboy did the same to the teenager in the passenger seat. Like his friend, he didn't have a gun. Leading him by the collar, Cowboy brought him around to the other side of the Bronco. "What were you doing back there?"

"None of your damn business, man," the driver said, trying to sound tough. "Who do you dudes think you are?"

Lyons shoved the muzzle of the M-16 under the nose of the driver, causing him to rise on his toes to maintain balance. "I'll ask the questions. You give the answers. Understand?"

"Hey, man, I've got my rights. I don't have to say nothin'."

Before the conversation went any further, Schwarz and Blancanales pulled up alongside the Bronco.

"Sorry we're late," Pol said, eyeing the two teenagers. "What we got here?"

"A couple of ACLU lawyers," Cowboy said with a laugh.

"I take it neither of these gentlemen are Queensbury," Gadgets said.

"Hey, you guys know Mr. Queensbury?" the driver asked.

"We're not what you'd call good friends," Pol said with a warm smile, "but we know him."

"One of you guys Carl Lyons?"

"The one pointing the gun at your face," Cowboy said.

"Gee, I'm sorry, Mr. Lyons, but we weren't sure who you were. We've got a message for you from Mr. Queensbury."

"What's the message?" Lyons said, lowering his weapon.

"It didn't make any sense to me, but he said you'd understand."

"What's the message?"

The driver shrugged. "He said to tell you that the clock's ticking. And you now have only forty-seven hours."

4

Hal Brognola was reading the computer printouts as fast as Aaron Kurtzman's computers could print them. He didn't like what he read. The meeting in Washington had been a disaster. Everyone from the CIA to the Coast Guard had been called to a special session at the Pentagon's war room. The President was taking the threat seriously: enough toxin had been stolen to kill over twenty million people. No one had known who had stolen the toxin or what would happen next until the note had arrived from Queensbury.

"This guy's nuts," Brognola stated flatly as he slapped one of the files with the back of his hand. "Absolutely nuts."

"It doesn't make him any less dangerous," Lyons said as he fell heavily into the only available chair and picked up one of the reports. Bear's lair was designed for one man and a wheelchair. With all of Able Team and Brognola present, there was barely room to inhale.

Kurtzman pushed away from one keyboard with the intention of rolling backward to another. Instead, he ran into Pol. "Get out of the way," he snapped.

"Sorry," Blancanales said as he cleared a path.

Brognola unwrapped a cigar and shoved it into his mouth. Known affectionately as the "head Fed," Brognola was the buffer between Stony Man and the Washington bureaucracy. He gave the men of Able Team—this antiterrorist fighting squad—their orders.

"How do you know this guy, Carl?" he asked as he chomped on the cigar.

"I arrested him when I was working Justice."

"That was a long time ago. Where's he been since then?"

"He stayed out of the gas chamber by pleading insanity. Since then he's been in a mental hospital."

Pol nudged Gadgets and said under his breath, "I guess Brognola was right—the guy's nuts."

"Put a sock in it, Blancanales," Brognola said. "There's too much at stake here. That lunatic has enough toxin to murder more people than both world wars killed."

"He's no lunatic," Lyons said softly. "Brilliant and totally evil, yes. But he's not crazy."

"You seem to know this guy pretty well, Ironman," Gadgets said as he leaned against the door frame.

"Too well." Lyons paced in a tight circle. "Herbert Queensbury has one of the highest IQs ever recorded."

"How high?" Gadgets asked.

"I don't remember exactly, but it was over two hundred."

"Wow, only a handful of people have ever tested that high."

"He graduated with a Ph.D. from MIT when he was twelve. He studied in Europe till he was eighteen, then came home to become a teacher at a small liberal arts college in southern Indiana."

"That's odd," Gadgets said. "I would have thought one of the Ivy League schools would have gobbled him up."

"They all tried, but he had his reasons for going to Monroe College."

"Oh! Monroe College." A sudden light of recognition flashed in Gadgets's eyes. "He's the guy who killed all those students."

"He caused their deaths, but he didn't kill them."

"Huh?" Pol said as he brought a handkerchief up to his nose.

Gadgets scratched his head. "They were playing some kind of a game if I remember correctly."

"Right. There's an elaborate set of tunnels that connect all the buildings on the Monroe Campus. He had the kids play a real-life fantasy game. The only problem was that the losers ended up dead."

"All of this is very interesting," Brognola said, chewing on his unlit cigar. "But we need to work on the current problem. Any ideas where to look for this Queensbury?"

"Everything's a game to this guy," Lyons said. "But he always plays fair and gives you a chance to win. That's how I managed to catch him. Last time he underestimated me and lost. I don't think he'll make the same mistake again."

"Oh?" Brognola said as he chomped even harder on his cigar. "Why do you say that?"

"Well," Lyons said as he pulled the original note from his pocket. "He said to bring my friends along. That means he knows about Able Team and is prepared to meet us head-to-head."

"Impossible," Brognola said with a snort. One of Brognola's main functions was to keep Stony Man out of the newspapers and away from Senate subcommittees. Stony Man wasn't supposed to exist.

"Look, Hal," Lyons said, "he knew where to find me to buzz me with the plane. I'd recommend that you conduct a full-scale security sweep of the Farm. Especially," Lyons added, glancing over at Kurtzman, who was toiling away on his keyboard, "the computer system."

"What!" Bear roared. "No one could tamper with my computers. They're one hundred percent secure."

"I'm sure they are," Lyons agreed. "But they're connected by phone wires to other data bases. He could be leaving your information alone but running duplicates of everything for himself. The man's a computer genius.''

''Bull,'' Kurtzman said as his fingers danced over the keyboard. ''If anyone's been tampering with—''

''What?'' Brognola demanded.

''Some of the computer files I use have a time and access record to show when it was activated and by whom. The log shows that whenever I pulled a file, it was pulled later by another system.''

''Let me guess who,'' Lyons said.

''The bastard even used my personal access codes,'' Kurtzman rasped.

''Wonderful,'' Brognola said as he spit fragments of his cigar on the floor. ''We've had a major breach of security and he knows we're onto him. What can we do about it, Bear?''

Kurtzman's expression was grim. His computers were his children. He wouldn't tolerate them being violated. ''I'll bury him with information. I'll order up files I don't need and overload his system. When I'm finished, it'll take twenty computer experts a month just to sift through the junk.''

''Good,'' Brognola said. ''Now for the next problem. Where do we find this guy?''

''He's already told us where to start our search,'' Lyons said.

''He has?''

"Yes." Lyons picked up the note from the Gamesmaster and looked at the label from the toxin bottle. "We start at BioTech Labs."

FRANK JUDSON, wearing blue jeans with a tool-laden belt around his waist, was rolling coaxial cable along the new floor. The return to the old mine was bittersweet. Judson had dropped out of high school and started mining coal when he was only sixteen. When the company decided it was more profitable to shut the old mine down than to fight the United Mine Workers, he found himself unemployed and unskilled. But in the eighteen years since the notice of closure had been tacked up on the mine's bulletin board, Judson had built a nice construction business.

"We're about done, Mr. Parker."

Herbert Queensbury nodded and checked his watch. "Excellent."

"Say," Judson asked as he rubbed a smudge of dirt from his face, "when will the camera crews arrive?"

"Next week," Queensbury said with a forced smile.

"We've never had a real Hollywood movie filmed around here before. Do you think they'll be needin' any extras?"

"I'm only in charge of special effects. The director handles all the casting."

Judson took off his yellow hard hat and wiped his forehead. The air in the cave was a constant fifty-four degrees, but Judson had been working hard enough to break a sweat. He wanted to impress the big shots from California. Work was hard to find these days, and the bonus for getting the wiring done early would come in really handy.

Queensbury handed Judson a check. "Tell your men thanks."

Judson examined the check before folding it into his front pocket. All of the other checks had been written from a local bank. This one was from the Bank of America's Burbank office. Judson wasn't surprised, considering the amount of the draft. His eyes sparkled. Two weeks' wages and overtime for his entire crew of seventeen, plus the early completion bonus. Those guys from Hollywood sure knew how to throw money around.

"You sure you don't need any help setting up the rest of your equipment?"

"No, my brother and his men can handle the rest." Queensbury rubbed his chin. "You could do one thing for me, though."

"Shoot, you name it, Mr. Parker."

"Pass the word that we'll be setting up some explosive charges and testing them over the weekend. If anyone hears any strange noises, tell them not to worry."

"Oh, sure, Mr. Parker, I understand."

"Also tell them, with all of the expensive equipment we've installed, there'll be an armed guard at the access road."

"No rubbernecking?"

"No rubbernecking."

"I'll pass the word."

"Thanks, Frank." Queensbury offered him his hand. "I'll mention you to the director."

"Gee, that'd be great, Mr. Parker." Frank Judson picked up his toolbox and headed for the exit. He whistled a country and western tune as he disappeared into the bowels of the cave.

Alfred Potts stepped from the shadows, chuckling. "That was great, Gamesmaster. Wait till he tries to cash that check."

Queensbury had found enough work to keep Judson underground until all the banks had closed. With tomorrow being Saturday, it would be Monday before he could possibly discover that the movie studio was a fake. By then Queensbury and his men would be long gone. And, with any luck, Carl Lyons would be dead.

"How much longer?" Queensbury asked.

"We can test the system anytime, Gamesmaster." Alfred Potts was nineteen years old, but his thin frame and acned complexion made him appear much younger. Queensbury had recruited him carefully. Brilliant but impressionable, Potts was the perfect assistant. He followed orders like a docile slave, never questioning. A wizard with electronics, he would serve as Queensbury's eyes and ears once Lyons and his friends entered the trap.

"Good, let's begin."

"Stand on the spot I marked," Potts said as he returned to the darkness.

Herbert Queensbury stepped up six inches to the elevated stage and found a place marked with two pieces of masking tape. "Here?"

"Yes," Potts said, his voice seeming to come from nowhere and everywhere.

Bright klieg lights blinked on, causing Queensbury to shield his eyes until they had time to adjust. "Does the light have to be so bright?"

"Yes," Potts answered from somewhere deeper in the cave. "It won't appear this bright to our visitors. Hold still while I focus." Potts stepped into the circle of light and began adjusting a camera that was on a tripod some twenty feet in front of Queensbury. "Once we start, you'll have a range of less than six inches or you'll be out of focus."

"I understand," Queensbury said as he shifted his weight uncomfortably. "How much longer will this take?"

"Let me just check the other two cameras, then we can test the system."

"Very well," Queensbury said with a sigh. There were a hundred things he would rather be doing, but this was the most important thing on his agenda at the moment. The video magic that Potts was capa-

ble of weaving was the key element of the game.
Without it, it would hardly be worth playing.

"All set."

"Good. Where are the rest of the men?"

"In the control center. Is there any chance Lyons
will arrive ahead of schedule?" Potts asked.

Herbert Queensbury shook his head. "No. Able
Team should be on its way to Iowa by now."

5

"I want a report within two hours of the time you land," Brognola said as he closed the door of the black Saberliner and stepped away. Jack Grimaldi, Stony Man's resident pilot, confirmed that the door was sealed before giving the sleek jet more power. The Saberliner roared down the Stony Man runway and in a wink was at thirty thousand feet and heading west.

"What's our ETA, Jack?" Lyons asked.

"Three hours."

Ironman's face told everyone he wasn't pleased with the answer. The clock was ticking. The countdown had started. He had forty-four hours to find the Gamesmaster; he didn't like wasting three of them in the back seat of an airplane.

"How'd you hook up with this Queensbury in the first place?" Gadgets asked, thumbing through the files in his lap.

"A Washington big shot's daughter was a student at Monroe College and she came up missing. The father called in a few markers, and I was sent to look for her.''

"Isn't Monroe some kind of special college?'' Gadgets asked.

"Yeah,'' Lyons answered. "They only accept gifted students and they charge an arm and a leg. Some of the students are as young as twelve. The girl I was looking for was a senior and only seventeen.''

"Did you find her?''

Lyons inhaled deeply and glanced out the window at the Appalachian Mountains. "I found her body,'' he said in a voice so soft that it was difficult to hear over the roar of the jet's engines.

"Queensbury killed her?''

"Yeah. The coroner's report called it a suicide. But he killed her just as sure as if he'd put a gun to her head and pulled the trigger.''

Gadgets and Pol exchanged glances. They both saw the pain in Lyons's ice-cold blue eyes. The stakes were high, but this mission was personal. Ironman would get Herbert Queensbury or die trying.

"There's no telling when we'll get another opportunity to sleep,'' Lyons said. "We'd better catch a few winks now.''

Pol and Gadgets nodded. Within five minutes all three men were asleep. Grimaldi glanced back and shook his head. "Only Able Team,'' he muttered under his breath, "could sleep at a time like this.''

AT THE SOUND of the landing gear going down, all three warriors instantly became alert. Lyons checked his watch, Blancanales flexed his jaw as he tried to relieve some of the pressure in his ears from his clogged head, and Gadgets rolled his shoulders and stretched. Through the windows they could see an airport surrounded by farmland.

"Where are we?" Lyons asked.

Grimaldi held up one finger as he spoke into a microphone. "I copy, Tower. We'll land on runway 101. This is SM 007 out." Grimaldi pivoted in his chair. "We're about ready to touch down. Buckle up."

The three men of Able Team did as directed and soon the black jet was on the ground. Lyons opened the door and was greeted by a burly man in a guard's uniform. Parked just to the right on the tarmac was a light blue four-door Ford with a row of police lights attached to the roof. Painted on the driver's door was the BioTech logo with Security in block letters underneath.

The guard extended his hand to Lyons. "George Wagner, chief of security at BioTech."

Ironman found the grip firm and dry. "Carl Lyons." He motioned over his shoulder. "Rosario Blancanales and Hermann Schwarz."

With the introductions out of the way, the four men headed toward the car. They stopped at the sound of Grimaldi's voice. "What do you want me to do, Ironman?'' The Stony Man pilot was now at the bottom of the steps of the Saberliner.

''Top off the tanks,'' Lyons answered. ''And be ready to leave on short notice.''

''Roger, dodger,'' Grimaldi answered with a smile.

Wagner took off his hat and placed it on the front seat next to Lyons. Pulling himself behind the wheel, he started the engine. ''I suppose you guys want to go to the plant.''

''Yes,'' Lyons answered. ''How long will it take to get there?''

''Five minutes. The site was selected because of its closeness to the airport.'' The Ford's engine idled roughly as they sat on the tarmac.

''Well,'' Lyons said with an impatient edge to his voice, ''let's go.''

''Right,'' Wagner said as he slammed the car into gear. For two days he'd had to play patty-cake with hotshot outsiders like these three. He was tired of answering the same stupid questions. He was tired of everyone from the local police to the FBI looking down their noses at him. Hell, he hadn't even been on duty when the toxin had been stolen. And tomorrow he would have to give the eulogy at two funerals for men he'd hired and trained. His tolerance for taking crap had just about reached its limit.

Wagner had filled out in the twenty-five years since he'd played middle linebacker at Iowa State. Now his six-four frame had to carry 280 pounds. He spent enough time out of doors so that his arms and legs were as strong as ever, but his waist had expanded fourteen inches since his college days. He'd been head of security for BioTech since the day it had opened.

"How did they get into the plant?" Lyons asked.

"They blew up the guard station with high explosives."

"That was the only security?"

Wagner glared at Lyons. "What in hell does that mean?"

"What? Am I speaking Chinese? Which word didn't you understand?"

"Why don't you kiss my—"

"Hey, guys," Blancanales said as he leaned over the seat to separate the two men, "we're on the same side here. Look, George I realize you've probably been jerked around pretty good the past couple of days. We're not here to second-guess anyone or try to point fingers. We just want to get the toxin back."

George Wagner's grip on the steering wheel was so tight that his knuckles were white. "The attack occurred in the middle of the night. We had two men on the gate and one inside making foot rounds. He was on the other side of the plant when the bomb went off."

"So he wasn't involved?" Pol asked softly.

"Yes and no. He's the one who called the police. Other than that, all he saw were taillights. They were in and out in less than six minutes."

"And they timed it so that the other guard was out of position?" Lyons asked.

"Could have been a coincidence," Wagner offered.

"With Queensbury nothing's a coincidence," Lyons muttered.

George Wagner took a sudden interest in Ironman. "You guys know who did this?"

Pol, his elbows resting on the front seat, shook his head. "Not me, him," Pol said, motioning toward Lyons. "He had a run-in with him a few years back."

Wagner glanced at Lyons. "I'd sure like to get my hands on that guy."

"Not as much as he would," Pol answered, motioning toward Lyons again. Ironman, his eyes locked on the road in front of them, said nothing. Politician was the member of Able Team who stroked the bruised egos of the other branches of law enforcement. He could talk his way and in and out of almost any situation. Lyons was a man of direct action. To Ironman the shortest distance between two points was the trajectory of a 9 mm parabellum.

The flat Iowa countryside rolled by as George Wagner acted as "scene of the crime" tour guide. "There," Wagner said, pointing at a narrow lane off the main highway, "that's where they found the van that was used when they attacked the lab."

"You want to stop, Ironman?" Pol asked.

Lyons shook his head. Queensbury wouldn't make it that easy. There would be a clue somewhere, but it wouldn't be in the van.

"The FBI went over it with a fine-tooth comb," Wagner said. "The only thing interesting they found were traces of human blood."

"Did one of the terrorists get shot?"

"The FBI guy didn't think so. It was just a trace of blood, like a nosebleed, but it was fresh. Here we are now." A makeshift gate had been constructed at the entrance to the BioTech facility. Two men, heavily armed, were at the gate. Someone had recently filled the crater created by the bomb with black asphalt; it contrasted starkly to the gray-white of the poured concrete driveway. "Dr. Stein said I should bring you directly to the lab."

"Who's Dr. Stein?"

"Head of the biological warfare division, and the inventor of the bug that was stolen."

A gust of warm air and the scent of burning rubber greeted the four men when they entered the laboratory.

"What's that smell?" Gadgets asked, curling his nose.

Pol looked puzzled. "What smell?"

"That's part of the building's security system," Wagner said as he reached for the handle of the second set of doors. "The air pressure in the building is balanced so that no air can escape unless it passes through the air filtration system. That lovely aroma is what air smells like when it's been heated up to two thousand degrees and run through charcoal filters.''

The inside of the building was white. The walls were white. The floor was white. The ceiling was white. The stench of the doorway was replaced with the odor of a strong disinfectant.

"You must give me the name of your decorator," Pol said as he surveyed the austere surroundings.

"Almost everything in here is white. It means that any dirt will show up at a glance. They've got some pretty nasty stuff in here." The four men walked down the corridor until they came to Dr. Stein's office. "Here we are, gentlemen." Wagner tucked his shirttail into his pants and adjusted his tie before rapping twice. Without waiting for a reply to his knock, the security man opened the door. "Dr. Stein, the men from Washington have arrived."

Gadgets's mouth fell open slightly and Blancanales smiled. Lyons was the only one who didn't seem to notice that Dr. Stein was a woman.

Gadgets and Pol knocked shoulders as they tried to be the first one to shake Nan Stein's hand. Pol, his reflexes slowed by his nagging cold, finished a close second.

"Gadgets Schwarz," he said as he extended his right hand.

At five-ten Nan Stein was exactly the same height as Gadgets. Her probing brown eyes were small and wide-spaced. Her nose was too large and her cheekbones too high for her oval face. Her raven black hair was pulled back into a bun. With the lithe, efficient build of a marathon runner, she had the dark complexion of a person who spent all of her free time outdoors. The mismatched features blended to make Nan Stein a very attractive person.

Dr. Stein let out a small sigh as she studied the men from Able Team. She wasn't impressed. "So you're the people everyone says can find my bug."

"We don't have a lot of time, ma'am," Lyons interjected. "Tell us about the weapon that was stolen."

"I've already told—"

"Tell it again," Lyons snapped.

Pol stepped between Lyons and Dr. Stein. "We need to know as much as we can as quickly as we can, Doctor." As always, Pol's voice was calm and soothing. "We already know who has your toxin. We need your help in locating him."

"You know who has it?"

"Yes."

"Who?"

"That doesn't matter," Lyons said, his eyes flashing with anger. "Just answer the questions."

Pol shot Ironman a look that would have frozen a blast furnace. "What my friend means is that any help you can give us would be greatly appreciated."

"First, tell us about the toxin," Gadgets began. "How does it work and does it require any special handling?"

"I'll explain how it works and then you can draw your own conclusions as to how it should be handled. The compound is in two parts. Each part by itself is totally harmless, but mixed together—"

"Mixed together it's fatal," Ironman said with a snort. "Can we have the condensed version of this story, please?"

"Mixed together it's still harmless," Dr. Stein answered tersely.

"Let her talk, Carl," Pol said softly. Ironman exhaled, his temper at the breaking point. He knew Pol was right. He also knew the clock was ticking.

"Please, Dr. Stein," Pol said graciously, "go on."

"The toxin is partially comprised of a dehydrated, gene-spliced derivative of the arum family of plants known as dieffenbachia. It's highly concentrated and extremely potent when mixed with a binder. Without a binder it can't bind to cells and is therefore totally harmless. The two parts, mixed dry, can still be handled without special equipment. However, once the two parts are rehydrated, they merge to form a very deadly toxin."

"How does it work?" Gadgets asked.

"It attacks the linings of the throat and nose of anyone who breathes it. The linings immediately become irritated and start to swell, eventually blocking the passages."

"They die of suffocation."

"Exactly, usually within ten minutes of contact."

"What's to stop it from killing friendly troops?" Gadgets asked.

"Nothing. Once the toxin becomes airborne, even the best gas mask won't keep it out. It's so small that it passes right through the filtration system."

"How is it controlled?"

"It can't be. It can only be avoided."

"Then how can the weapon be used?"

"The binder is made from organic material. After twenty-four hours it begins to break down. Exposure to ultraviolet light will also cause the compound to break down."

"What type of delivery system is used?"

"Rain or snow."

"You're kidding?" Gadgets said, the amazement showing in both his voice and face.

"No. The toxin is mixed together and dumped into the clouds on the leading edge of a storm front. The moisture activates the toxin, and wherever the rain falls, it falls."

"And twenty-four hours later troops can march in and begin burying the dead," Gadgets said softly.

Dr. Stein nodded grimly.

"Okay," Lyons said. "So as long as we don't spill coffee on the stuff, it's safe, right?"

Dr. Stein shook her head and looked at Schwarz. "Is your friend always like this?"

"Naw," Gadgets said with a warm smile. "This is one of his better days. You should see him when he's really being a jerk."

"No thanks."

"I want to see where the toxin was stored," Lyons said, ignoring the comments about his etiquette.

The security warehouse had been left undisturbed and off-limits since the raid. Lyons, on his haunches, examined the detached vault door.

Gadgets shook his head as he fiddled with one of the ruptured hinges. "Whoever did this really knew what he was doing." Pol and Ironman had to agree.

Lyons motioned for George Wagner. The big man lumbered over. "How many people knew what was in this vault?"

"Well," Wagner said, scratching his head. "I imagine just about everyone who worked here knew there was something off-limits in this vault."

"I mean," Lyons began impatiently, "how many people knew exactly what was in here?"

"I can answer that," Dr. Stein said as she joined the conversation. "Only ten people in this facility knew what we were making. And five more at the Pentagon."

"I want to see all ten of the BioTech people who knew about the toxin."

"Right," Wagner said. "I'll need a list, Dr. Stein."

"Of course. One's not here. My lab assistant, Kevin Pitts. He called in sick today."

"Sick?" Lyons said with sudden interest.

"Yes, he talked to my secretary this morning. She said he sounded awful. She didn't even recognize his voice. Said he had some kind of twenty-four-hour bug."

6

"I'm going with you," Dr. Stein said, her arms folded across her chest. "And that's the end of this discussion."

Lyons glared at the tall microbiologist, but said nothing.

"Come on, Ironman," Gadgets coaxed.

"Ironhead, if you ask me," muttered Nan Stein to herself.

"She knows where this Pitts guy lives and," Gadgets continued, smiling at Dr. Stein, "I don't think she's going to take no for an answer."

"I don't care if she comes or not," Lyons barked. "Let's go."

Gadgets took the middle of the back seat with Blancanales and Dr. Stein on either side. At first Pol thought Gadgets was just being gallant by offering to sit on the hump, then he realized he'd been suckered. It was obvious that both men found Dr. Stein extremely attractive. Gadgets had managed to sit where he could monopolize her attention.

"I find it hard to believe that Kevin would be involved with anything like this."

Lyons pivoted around from the front seat. "Let me describe Kevin Pitts. He's young and brilliant."

"Amazing," Stein said, the sarcasm dripping from every word. "A scientist who's smart. You could do a Las Vegas lounge act reading minds."

"He loves science fiction or fantasy stories and probably attends *Star Trek* conventions."

Dr. Stein fell silent, her attitude subdued.

"He has few friends and his favorite pastime is playing Dungeons and Dragons."

"How do you know all of this?"

"He's worked for BioTech for less than a year."

"Six months."

"And you almost didn't hire him because you were afraid he was overqualified."

"Yes, but—"

"He's been a model employee and an invaluable assistant."

"You've read Kevin's file."

"No," Lyons answered quietly. "I've read the obituaries of half a dozen other smart kids just like him."

"My God," Stein said, clutching her throat. "Do you think Kevin's dead?"

Lyons didn't answer; he didn't have to. His eyes supplied the answer she didn't want to hear.

"We don't know for sure," Gadgets said gently as he patted the shaken woman on the knee.

"He's right. Kevin's probably already dead."

Gadgets had expected more emotion from the pretty scientist after her initial reaction. Yet now she was discussing the possible death of a co-worker as calmly as the demise of a laboratory rat. She read the puzzled look in Gadgets's eyes.

"I don't cry for the dead anymore, Mr. Schwarz."

"Call me Gadgets."

"Only if you'll call me Nan."

"Thanks, Nan. I have one question...."

"What's a nice girl like me doing in this kind of business?"

Gadgets tried to conceal a sheepish grin. "Something like that."

"My grandparents died in a Nazi concentration camp. My father was killed on the West Bank during the Six Day War in 1967. I was only twelve at the time and living on a kibbutz. My mother had died in childbirth, my birth, so that left just me and my brother. He tried to raise me with the help of the people in the kibbutz. But he was killed during the Yom Kippur War in 1973. I emigrated to the U.S. and lived with a distant aunt and uncle while I got my college degree."

"I still don't see..."

Nan rested her hand on Gadgets's knee. "Let me finish." She made no attempt to move her hand.

"Unlike most of the people I went to college with, I had seen death and terrorism firsthand. I understand that there's good and evil in this world. I also understand that sometimes good has to stand and fight. It's easy to say give peace a chance, but sometimes peace requires superior firepower."

"Were you ever in the military?"

"I served for two years in the Israeli army before going on to grad school."

"You're quite a woman."

Nan flashed a warm smile. "You're not so bad yourself."

KEVIN PITTS LIVED in a two-story clapboard frame house from which the white paint was badly peeling. Located in a quiet, tree-lined neighborhood of homes of similar design, the house had all the earmarks of a rental property with an absentee landlord. The flower beds were choked with weeds and the grass was several inches higher than any of the other lawns on the street. A broken shutter from a second-floor window was leaning against the side of the house and a new aluminum ladder was on the ground next to it. Kevin Pitts's car, along with two days worth of newspapers, was in the driveway.

The steps creaked as Able Team, Dr. Stein and George Wagner made their way up onto the porch. All of the blinds were pulled and the front door was locked tight. No one answered either the ringing of the bell or Ironman's heavy knocks.

"Go around and check the rear door, Pol."

Blancanales nodded and disappeared around the house. He returned a few moments later. "Locked and no sign of life."

Gadgets reached into his pants pocket and brought out a set of lock picks. Nan sent Gadgets a somewhat disapproving look.

"Advantages of a misspent youth, my dear." Before his hand reached the knob, Lyons grabbed his wrist and pulled him back. "What the . . . ?"

"I don't like it," Lyons rasped. "Let's go in a different way. Try all the windows."

Every window on the first floor was locked. Lyons walked off the porch and studied the house.

"What's the problem?" Nan whispered to Gadgets.

"I'm not sure, but Carl knows this Queensbury better than anyone and I think he smells a trap."

"That's it," Ironman said as he bolted toward the side of the house. Extending the aluminum ladder, he leaned it against the window with the missing shutter and headed up. The window was unlocked. Ironman disappeared inside. Two agonizing minutes passed before he reappeared at the window. "Gadgets, I need you. Pol, move everyone back."

Gadgets sprinted up the ladder and entered what was probably Kevin Pitts's bedroom. A mattress without a frame was on the floor and the ceiling and walls were covered with bizarre fantasy posters.

"Very nice," Gadgets said as he surveyed the room. "You find Pitts?"

"Yeah." Ironman led the way to the steps. "Be careful about what you touch. The whole house is booby-trapped."

Halfway down the steps, Gadgets caught the scent. Once the smell was logged in a person's memory bank it was never forgotten—the unmistakable odor of decaying human flesh.

Enough light sneaked into the room from around the edges of the curtains that Gadgets could make out Kevin Pitts tied to a chair in the middle of the living room. Tiny petechial blotches covered his face like hundreds of purple pinpricks. He had been dead long enough that the death gases of cell degeneration had expanded and bloated his body. Schwarz was mesmerized by the bulging eyes that threatened to leap from their sockets and the protruding tongue that had swollen to the size of a man's fist.

"Look at the doors and windows."

Gadgets forced himself to look away from the body of Kevin Pitts and focus his attention on the front door. A cold shiver ran down Schwarz's spine. If he had opened the door, Able Team and Dr. Stein would have been red smudges on the house across the street.

A trip wire was attached to the door frame and a satchel of plastic explosives lay a few inches behind the door. In Gadgets's haste to impress Nan Stein with his burglary skills he had gotten sloppy. Normally his internal alarm system would have gone off long before he had reached into his pocket for his lock pick. Fortunately Ironman hadn't been distracted.

"Can you disarm them?"

"Them?" Gadgets answered with a puzzled look on his face.

Ironman pointed at the windows. Each had a similar bomb attached.

"The window we used was the only way in without setting off the explosives?"

Lyons nodded. "That was why Queensbury left the ladder for us to find. He's devious, but he always plays fair."

"I can't wait to meet this guy."

"Let's hope it's soon."

Gadgets gingerly flipped back the lid of the satchel near the door. "Ironman, take a look at this."

Lyons peered inside the leather bag. Along with nearly three pounds of plastic explosives was a handwritten note.

Congratulations! Once again you've proven yourself a worthy opponent. If you remove the red wire from each of the packages of explosives, they'll be disarmed.

　　　　　　　　　　　　Sincerely,
　　　　　　　　　　　　The Gamesmaster

"What do you think?" Gadgets asked.

Lyons nodded.

Schwarz's fingers located the red wire that was attached to the detonator. He gave it a tug. A loud explosion and a flash of light from behind forced them to dive for cover. Both men were momentarily stunned by the percussion and the blinding flash.

"What was that?"

"Flash grenade. We'll be okay in a few minutes," Ironman assured Gadgets.

"Hey, you guys all right?" Pol shouted from the porch.

"Yeah," Lyons answered. "Don't touch that door! We'll let you in in a few minutes. Until then, clear the area and keep the neighbors back."

"Right!"

A blue haze of smoke settled in over the room, and slowly Gadgets and Ironman absorbed the shock to their sensory systems. Gadgets located the flash grenade and discovered that it had a radio-controlled firing mechanism that was triggered when he pulled the red wire. He also found another note.

Don't get cocky just because you've found your way through the first part of the maze. Many dangers lie ahead.

The Gamesmaster

"You know," Gadgets said as he handed the note to Lyons, "I'm really starting to dislike this Gamesmaster."

"WHAT HAPPENED? Are they all right?" Nan asked Pol as he sprinted back down the sidewalk.

"They're fine. I don't know what happened." Blancanales looked around the quiet neighborhood. The explosion inside Kevin Pitts's house had caused many people to walk out onto their porches in housecoats and slippers to see what had happened. Pol would have to do something fast or a crowd would form in front of the house. His eyes turned toward George Wagner's car. "Does that have a public address system?"

"Sure does," Wagner said, opening the car door.

"Hit the lights and hand me the microphone." Alternating rows of blue and white strobes flashed along the roof of the car.

"May I have your attention please?" Pol said into the microphone. "We've had a small gas line rupture. The noise you heard was an explosion inside this house. We have the situation *basically* under control. There's still a risk of additional explosions. Please, for your personal safety, return to your homes and stay inside."

"Should we evacuate the area?" a man in a soiled white T-shirt and sweatpants shouted from across the street.

"That won't be necessary at this time. Just stay inside."

Pol handed the microphone back to George Wagner. "Every couple of minutes announce that everyone should remain indoors."

Wagner smiled. "Real cute. But you've still got one problem."

"What's that?"

"It just came in over my radio. Somebody called the police. They should be here any minute."

"I just hope no one from the press has their Bearcat scanner on. We can handle the police, but a nosy reporter is another matter entirely."

"You can come in now," Gadgets shouted from the front porch. "The building is secured."

Nan sprinted down the sidewalk and up the steps. "Are you all right?"

"My ears are ringing, but other than that I'm fine." Gadgets lowered his eyes and his voice. "I'm afraid I can't say the same for Pitts."

"Dead?"

Schwarz nodded.

"I want to see the body."

"Why?"

"To see if he was killed with my toxin."

"It's not pretty," Gadgets warned.

Nan shook her head slowly. "I have to know."

Lyons had removed all the lamp shades in the living room to increase the amount of available light as he searched for more booby traps. In the stark light the body of Kevin Pitts appeared even more ghastly.

"What's she doing in here?" Lyons asked crossly.

"She wants to see the body," Gadgets told him.

Nan surprised both Gadgets and Ironman. Her face registered neither shock nor horror. Instead, she approached Pitts like a coroner about to perform the fourth autopsy of the day. She examined the body with clinical detachment. Moving in, she lifted his head by the chin with one finger.

"He was definitely killed by the toxin," she pronounced with calm certainty. "He died of suffocation, but there are no marks on the throat except for internal swelling."

"What about the red marks on his face?"

"Petechiae. It's caused when the small blood vessels near the surface of the skin hemorrhage from the strain of trying to breathe."

"Hey, what's going on in here?" a male voice asked from the doorway. All eyes turned to see a young policeman with his right hand on the butt of his revolver. When he saw the body, his eyes grew large. "Dear God," he muttered as he bolted for the handrail of the porch with his hand over his mouth.

"We don't have much time," Lyons said. "We have to find the next clue before more police arrive and seal off the building."

"What's this?" Nan asked as she pointed at a piece of paper tucked into the dead man's front shirt pocket.

Gadgets reached for the paper. "It's another note, Ironman. And again it's addressed to you."

7

Carl Lyons read the note out loud for the second time. "Give me a call. The Gamesmaster." He shook his head. "Call him where? What phone number do we use?" Ironman frowned as he ran his fingers through his hair.

"Let me have a look," Gadgets said as he relieved Lyons of the note. Before he had time to examine the message, though, there was a commotion on the front porch.

"Get out of my way!" a barrel-chested police sergeant ordered as he shoved Blancanales out of his path. "What in hell happened here? Who are you people?"

"Pol," Lyons barked, "handle this."

"I'm trying, Ironman. I'm trying." Pol put his arm around the cop's shoulder and tried to steer him out of the house and back to the porch. "Look, Sarge," Pol said, "just make one phone call to this number and—"

"Get your hands off me or I'll have you arrested."

Pol pulled his hands away and held them up in mock surrender. "Just call this number or call your chief. That way you'll know what's going on."

"That's it!" Gadgets shouted from the other side of the room. "Where's the phone?"

"Hey, don't touch anything else, you jerk," the cop yelled as he marched back into the center of activity.

"What is it? What have you got?" Ironman demanded.

"Maybe nothing, maybe everything," Gadgets said as he reached for the phone.

"I said not to touch anything else," the police sergeant ordered.

"Pol," Lyons growled, "shut him up."

Pol shrugged. "Okay, Sarge," he said as he pulled his Uzi pistol from under his left arm and pressed it into the policeman's ribs, "we're going to walk out to your car and get on the radio and talk to your boss."

The cop looked down at the nasty black weapon and slowly raised his hands. "You're in big trouble."

"Naw, it's just a cold. I'll be fine in a few days." Using the barrel of the Uzi to point the way, Pol guided the policeman out the door.

Lyons watched as Gadgets punched a series of numbers on the phone—42637627837. "Whose phone number is that?"

"If I'm right, it'll be the Gamesmaster's." Schwarz held the phone where both he and Ironman could hear any conversation that took place. The phone rang only once.

"Hello, Carl."

The hair on Ironman's neck bristled. He recognized the voice. It was Herbert Queensbury.

"I'm going to find you," Lyons said softly.

"I must admit that you're doing much better than I had expected. I really must be going."

"Wait."

"Oh, how foolish of me. You want your next clue. Go back upstairs and look behind the poster." The line went dead.

Lyons bolted for the stairs and Kevin Pitts's bedroom. Within two minutes he had found the hand-written note taped to the back of a poster of the heavy metal rock group Twisted Sister. He read it once and handed it to Gadgets, who read it out loud. "Almost heaven, where New is old."

Gadgets passed the note along to Nan. She shrugged and handed it back. "I have no idea what this means."

"Unfortunately, I do. When I caught Queensbury the first time, he used rhymes as clues. It's a game within a game. We have to find the other part of the rhyme to find Queensbury."

"Where do we start?" Gadgets asked.

Ironman's eyes locked onto a school pennant hanging over Kevin Pitts's bed. "I have a good idea."

Gadgets followed Ironman's eyes to the blue-and-gold pennant.

Monroe College.

"COME ON, JACK," Lyons said as he gave Stony Man's pilot a rough shake.

Grimaldi, curled up in the pilot's seat of the Saberliner, rubbed his eyes and stretched. "What time is it?" he asked, suppressing a yawn.

"It's nearly four." With all the stars twinkling in the clear Iowa sky, Lyons knew Grimaldi didn't have to ask if it was a.m. or p.m. "How soon can we be in the air?"

"Where are we going?"

"Madison, Indiana."

"Never heard of it," the Stony Man pilot said as he reached for a map. "Does it have an airport?"

"Couldn't tell you. It's about halfway between Louisville and Cincinnati on the Ohio River."

Jack Grimaldi flipped on a light above his seat and studied the map more closely. "They have an airport, but it doesn't have a control tower."

"Meaning?" Lyons asked.

"Meaning, we'll be there in about two hours." Grimaldi glanced over his shoulder as Nan Stein buckled herself into one of the rear seats. "Who's the woman and why is she here?"

Gadgets took care of the introductions and explained that her help might be needed to neutralize the toxin.

Reading Schwarz's eyes, he saw the obvious attraction the Able Team warrior had for the woman. A mischievous smile crept over Grimaldi's face. "If you say so, Gadgets. Oh, I almost forgot," he said as he reached under the front seat. "You got a care package from Bear." Grimaldi flipped a courier's pouch in the general direction of Schwarz. Like a good infielder, Gadgets moved quickly to his right and caught the parcel on the short hop.

"Bear?" Nan asked, knitting her eyebrows.

"Aaron Kurtzman," Gadgets told her.

"Heavyset, dark, confined to a wheelchair?"

"Yeah, you know him?" Gadgets asked as he broke the seal on the pouch.

"We've never been formally introduced, but we attended the same seminar a few years back."

"What is it, Gadgets?" Lyons asked.

Schwarz thumbed through an inch-thick stack of papers. "Information about Queensbury and—" Gadgets suddenly stopped talking and moved one of the files to the bottom of the stack.

"Hold it, buster," Nan said as she reached for the file Gadgets was trying to conceal. "I saw that."

"Sorry," Gadgets said with a sheepish grin as he handed the file to the microbiologist.

"What's that?" Pol asked as he reached for his handkerchief. Nan held the file up so that Blancanales could read the label; it had her name printed on top. "Oh," he said just before making a noise like a Canada goose. "Sorry, but I have to get my head cleared before we take off. The change in air pressure is murder on the ears."

"Here you go, Pol," Grimaldi said as he flipped him a pack of gum. "Chew a couple of pieces. It'll help."

"How long before we can leave?" Lyons asked as he checked his watch.

"Well," Grimaldi began, "I'll need to make a few quick phone calls. I'm not sure the airport at Madison will handle a plane this large. We may have to land at the Jefferson Proving Ground."

"How far away is that from Madison?"

"About twenty miles north."

"Close enough. Let's go."

Gadgets had been watching Nan as she read the file. Her cheeks were flushed and her breath came in short gulps. "I can't believe this!" she finally said as she turned the page. "This has everything about me except my bra size."

Gadgets pretended to flip through the file, then looked up and said. "Here it is on page seven. 34B."

Nan shook her head and sneered. "Watch it."

Gadgets's only answer was a smile. The contents of the pouch had been passed around like the Sunday paper at a family reunion. Everyone except Grimaldi was reading a section.

"Wow," Pol said softly as he read a section of Queensbury's file. "This is amazing."

"What?" Lyons asked from the copilot's seat.

"The way Queensbury escaped from prison."

"How'd he do it?" Gadgets asked as he tried to sneak Nan's file off her lap. But she slapped his hands away and continued reading.

Pol cleared his throat. "For a while he was being held in a maximum-security prison and was a model inmate. He was transferred to a minimum-security facility in Pennsylvania where they had a computer training program for the inmates."

"Damn," Lyons muttered under his breath. "That's like giving a homicidal maniac a loaded gun."

"It gets better," Pol said, flipping to the next page in the file. "Apparently the computer had a modem that allowed him to contact people outside. He hooked into one of those information-sharing networks and made some friends on the outside."

"And they helped him escape," Lyons said with disgust.

"Well, sort of," Pol answered. "Actually, technically he didn't escape."

"What's in that bottle of nose spray, Pol?" Gadgets asked.

"I'm serious," Pol answered defensively. "Apparently one of the people from his computer network hacked his way into the prison's computer system and changed the files on Queensbury."

"And?" Lyons asked impatiently.

"And," Pol answered, "they let him go."

"What!" Ironman shouted. "They just opened up the front gate and let him out?"

"They thought he had served his complete sentence. But it gets better. Apparently while he was in minimum security he used the same computer trick to have four convicts released from Joliet." A thin whistle escaped from Schwarz's lips. "Not exactly the kind of guys I'd want my sister to date. Here, read it for yourself." Pol handed Lyons the folder.

Ironman's cold blue eyes scanned the pages. The anger and frustration turned his face to stone.

Nan studied Ironman with interest. She leaned over and whispered in Gadgets's ear, "Your friend is kind of scary."

"Don't worry. He's had his shots."

"Hey, Gadgets," Pol said, turning his attention away from Lyons, "how did you figure out what number to call to **get** Queensbury?"

"Well," the electronics whiz answered, "his note said to give him a call. I pushed the numbers on the dial that corresponded with the letters in Gamesmaster. G is 4, A is 2, M is 6 and so on."

"Why can't we just trace the phone number and find Queensbury?"

"It wasn't a real number. There were eleven digits. The phone had an open line to Queensbury, but it needed the proper code entered to activate the connection."

"Oh." Pol flexed his jaw and tried to clear his ears. It didn't help, so he reached for his handkerchief again. "What do you make of the first clue?"

"Almost heaven, where New is old." Gadgets scratched his head. "I haven't got the slightest idea."

Nan shrugged, and Pol held up his hands in mock surrender. Ironman ignored the chatter, focusing his attention on the folder on his lap. Included in the file was a recent photograph of Herbert Queensbury. Lyons couldn't take his eyes off the black-and-white photo. It brought back memories he'd hoped he'd forgotten. In his careers as an L.A. cop, special agent and a member of Able Team he had seen and done many things that haunted his sleep. The worst nightmares always had Queensbury lurking in them.

Lyons lifted the photo out of the file. This battle was personal. Queensbury versus Lyons. The stakes were too high for Ironman to even consider the prospect of losing.

"I beat you once before," the blond warrior said quietly to the photograph. "And I'll beat you again."

8

A strong low pressure center in the Gulf of Mexico had pumped an unseasonable gust of warm, moist air over the Ohio River valley. For two days a light drizzle had fallen. Even at 5:00 a.m. the temperature still hovered above the freezing mark. The radio weather report said a cold blast was quickly moving in from Canada. Paul Moore knew he would have to be careful on the bridges and overpasses; they would freeze before the highways. He was glad he had decided to lock out the hubs on his four-wheel-drive Bronco before he had left the farm.

Moore tapped the button for his wipers. The windshield was coated with something between rain and sleet. The midwinter soup got thicker the closer he got to the Ohio River. From experience he knew the bridge at Madison, Indiana, would be completely blanketed by fog until the morning sun had a chance to burn it off. Moore flipped on the yellow fog lights under his front bumper and shook his head.

He had been waiting for the phone call for months. The FBI had informed him of Herbert Queensbury's escape, and he knew it was only a matter of time before the bastard returned to Monroe College.

Moore had been a part-time security guard when the first Queensbury episode had exploded in the national headlines. Six students, one only fifteen years old, had died in a bizarre game devised by the twisted genius. The college, fearing the loss of alumni support and a decline in enrollment, had tried to sweep the incident under the rug. With that high a body count, the cover-up quickly unraveled. The college president and Moore's boss were both fired. The board of directors needed someone squeaky clean to take over the job of head of security, so they chose Paul Moore.

A sergeant in the Green Berets, Moore had returned to his family's farm in Trimble County, Kentucky, hoping to put the ugliness of Vietnam behind him. He had quickly enrolled in classes at nearby Monroe College on the GI Bill.

Moore had hoped to melt into the campus, get a degree and do a little farming. Instead, he had stood out like a sore thumb. Six-two and a lean one-ninety, his military haircut was the giveaway. To the long-haired students on campus he was a freak. A Neanderthal. Someone to be avoided at all costs. That was fine with Moore; he needed the time and space to sort out his place in the world in post-Vietnam America.

He had done what he'd felt was right by enlisting. He had put his body on the line so that the snot-nosed kids at Monroe could burn their draft cards and chant antiwar slogans. He hadn't expected a brass band and a parade when he came home. He hadn't expected to be spit on, either.

Moore checked his watch. He had nearly an hour before Lyons and his group would touch down. He decided to take a swing around the campus before heading out to the Jefferson Proving Ground.

The business district of the historic river town was bathed in a dull yellow glow from ancient gas streetlamps. Moore's was the only vehicle on the road, but he waited for the red light to change at the intersection of U.S. 421 and State 56. Most of the white frame homes that dotted the hillside overlooking Main Street were dark. In a few the kitchen lights were on as sleepy housewives made the first pot of morning coffee.

Moore turned left on State Route 7 and headed toward the campus of Monroe College. The narrow, winding road made its way up to the top of the bluffs overlooking Madison. Thin sheets of ice were starting to form on the faces of the cut stone on the hillside. Long icicles hung like daggers from the rocks. The county road crew had already salted the road, and the oversize tires of Moore's Bronco easily held the asphalt.

As Moore slowed to a stop at the guarded gate to the main entrance of the campus, Johnny Johnson stepped out of the small guardhouse and slapped his hands together. "Hey, Paul," he said with a smile, "what brings you out on such a rotten morning?"

"Couldn't sleep," he lied. Moore knew that Johnny had a big mouth. If he told him why he was there, every security man on campus would know the reason within an hour, even if it meant getting a few of them out of bed. "Any action tonight?"

"Naw," Johnson said, stomping his feet. "Damn, it's getting colder by the minute."

"Snowing like hell up in Chicago. It should hit here in a few hours."

"Great! By then I'll be home and in bed."

"Drive careful. The roads are starting to get bad."

"Oh, one thing did happen tonight."

"Let me guess—old lady Creasley."

"Right."

"Normal complaint?"

"Yup."

"You check it out?"

"Yup."

"Anything?"

"Nope. Never is. I don't think the old biddy's playing with a full deck. Since the word got out that Queensbury was on the loose, every time a student walks by her house she calls us."

"Yeah," Moore agreed. "She can be a real pain. I'll talk to you later, Johnny."

Moore rolled up the window and drummed his fingers on the steering wheel. Mrs. Creasley was a real pain. Her house was located right next to the old power plant, the center of action the last time Queensbury had been in town. Now, every time she heard a bump in the night, she called campus security.

What if this time she was right?

Moore sighed as he threw the Bronco into reverse and headed toward the old power plant. Mrs. Creasley's house, a well-kept Victorian clapboard built by a river captain when Madison was a boomtown, was only sixty yards from the old power plant. From her rear window she could keep track of any activity near the building. Since her husband had been killed in a freak boating accident in 1972, she had acted as the unofficial guardian of the south end of the campus. Unfortunately, when she had noticed suspicious activity around the abandoned power plant years earlier, her warnings had fallen on deaf ears. If the school had listened to her instead of taking her for a crank, the entire Queensbury incident might have been avoided.

Moore pulled his Bronco into one of the three parking spaces in front of the squat white buildings. The snow had started to fall in earnest, and even from less than ten yards it was difficult to make out any details of the building. Now only used by the maintenance department for storage, the plant had once generated all of the heat for every building on campus. In its basement were two massive boilers that had produced the steam that pumped through a maze of underground tunnels to the other buildings on campus. A new, more efficient power plant had been built in the late sixties. Since the old one was tucked away on a far corner of the campus, it had been easier to find other uses for the building than to tear it down.

Moore was fumbling in his glove compartment for his set of building keys when he caught movement out of the corner of his eye. Someone darted from behind a tree to the rear of the building. Moore jumped from his truck while grabbing his hand-held walkie-talkie.

"Johnny!" Moore shouted into the transmitter as he tried to catch up with the fleeing person.

"Yeah?" came the scratchy reply.

"We've got some kids playing around the old power plant. Get a couple of men and get over here."

"Right."

The person he was chasing had disappeared into the blowing swirl of white. Moore took off in a trot, following the footprints in the snow. Whoever he was chasing had small feet. Turning the corner to the rear of the building, he saw a young woman scrambling to get into an open rear window.

"Stop!" Moore shouted. "Campus Security!"

The girl, her eyes wide with terror, dropped the bag she was carrying and dived headfirst into the window. Moore slowed his pace. He had no chance of catching her before she reached the tunnels, and once she'd made it that far there were a thousand hiding places. Without a flashlight and a map, Moore knew he wouldn't get ten yards before having to turn back.

He bent over and picked up the bag the girl had dropped. It was heavy. "Damn!" Moore muttered under his breath as he straightened. The snow on the ground around the window had been packed solid. He could make out at least two distinctive sets of footprints; there might have been more, but it was impossible to tell.

The security chief shook his head as he opened the brown paper bag. A cold chill, which had nothing to do with the weather, cut him to the bone.

The nightmare had started again.

"THIS OUGHT TO BE INTERESTING," Grimaldi said as the Saberliner banked over the landing strip at the Jefferson Proving Ground.

"Is there a problem?" Lyons asked from the passenger section.

"Naw. There's about two inches of snow on the runway and a forty-mile-per-hour crosswind."

Lyons looked out the pilot's window. If there was an airstrip out there, he couldn't see it. All he could see was white. "You sure about this?"

"Piece of cake."

"Do you think it would be better to land in Indianapolis or Louisville?" Lyons asked.

"They're both closed."

"Wonderful," Blancanales said as he reached for a tissue to clear his nose.

"Everyone buckle up," Grimaldi said brightly. The Jefferson Proving Ground had made the Pentagon hit list of military installations to be closed. For thirty years the congressman from southern Indiana had traded his vote on other issues to keep the obsolete base open. But it did have a decent landing strip, certainly long enough for the Saberliner, and a radar-controlled tower. Even in this weather Grimaldi was confident.

Nan Stein was sorry she had talked her way onto the plane. Her fingernails dug into the armrest of her seat. Her face was as white as the snow outside. Gadgets placed his hand on top of hers, causing her to jump.

"Relax," he said gently. "Jack's the best in the business. If anyone can bring this bad boy down safely, it's him."

The doctor forced a smile, but her mouth was too dry to answer.

The nose of the black bird began to angle downward. The closer it got to the ground, the more it was buffeted by the near-blizzard conditions. Grimaldi had to make numerous adjustments with the controls to keep the Saberliner on its proper glide path.

At six hundred feet they dropped out of the low-hanging clouds, and in the distance, closing fast, were the flashing strobes of the runway approach. The runway was completely covered with snow.

"Hang on tight, boys and girls. Here we go!"

The Saberliner hit the runway with a dull thud that caused Nan to gasp. When all three legs of the landing gear were on the ground, Grimaldi tapped the brakes. The plane started to slide. Grimaldi released the brake and hit the throttle, straightening out the jet.

"Solid ice underneath," he reported.

"How are we going to stop?" Nan demanded.

The jet rumbled down the runway, and the far tree line was closing at a frightening speed. Grimaldi threw the airplane's engines into full reverse. The jets screamed in protest, and the plane shook as if the wings were about to fall off. Then the jet began to slow down, but not fast enough to avoid the trees at the end of the runway.

"Bat turn," Grimaldi shouted as he applied the left side brakes. The jet went into an immediate spin but didn't flip. Nan screamed while Pol blew his nose again.

The plane corkscrewed off the runway like a drunken ice skater. The soil underneath the snow hadn't frozen yet, and the weight of the plane caused the wheels to sink six inches into the turf. The plane jerked to a halt sixty feet off the runway and only two hundred yards from a thick stand of beech trees.

"See," Grimaldi said. "Piece of cake."

9

"Holy..." Paul Moore muttered to himself as he watched the Saberliner spin off the runway. Slamming the Bronco into gear, he headed in a straight line toward the airplane. The four-wheel-drive Ford bumped onto an unpaved section that separated the parking lot from the runway, and the oversize tires immediately began to sink into the wet, unfrozen turf. He gunned the engine. Mud spun off his wheels and left a brown trail in the falling snow. A siren wailed in the distance, and the flashing lights of emergency vehicles penetrated the gloom.

It took Moore less than thirty seconds to get to the disabled aircraft. Lyons already had the door of the plane open and was busy extending the built-in steps.

"You okay?" Moore shouted as he stepped from the Ford.

"Fine," Ironman answered, jumping out of the jet.

The two men shook hands with little enthusiasm. It was nothing personal. They had gone through an experience together that both would rather forget; seeing each other again was an unpleasant reminder.

"I have to admit I'm not too delighted to see you."

"Under the circumstances," Ironman said, nodding, "I have to agree."

"I've got some bad news." Moore handed Ironman the paper bag. "A kid dropped this outside the old power plant."

Lyons opened the bag, looked inside and shook his head. "Here we go again."

"What's in the bag, Ironman?" Blancanales asked as he stepped from the plane. Instead of answering, Lyons turned the bag over to Pol, who looked inside. "Lovely," he said as he passed it along to Gadgets.

"What is it?" Nan asked as she joined the others.

"Just your everyday bag of goodies from the local terrorist shop. Let's see," Gadgets said as he began removing items from the sack. "We have six, count 'em, six hand grenades. Three percussion, three flash. This is interesting. Your standard-issue tranquilizer pistol with two dozen darts..."

"Let me see one of the darts," Nan said with urgency in her voice. The dart was about three inches long and contained a tin vial of a blue liquid that would be injected into the victim upon impact.

"Is it the toxin?" Blancanales asked.

Nan shook her head.

"That's too bad," Lyons said as he zipped up his heavy coat.

"Why?" Nan asked.

"That means Queensbury isn't here."

CONNIE MANLEY BEAMED. "It went exactly as planned."

Professor Dan Ackerman smiled at the girl who was less than half his age. "Was there ever a doubt?" he asked as he reached for the phone. Ackerman, a tenured professor of Asian Studies, was roughly the size and shape of a small bear. It seemed as if every inch of the man was covered with black fur. A full beard, bushy eyebrows and a huge mound of permed hair covered his head. Even the backs of his hands were coated in black.

Manley, lithe and small-boned, pushed her stringy blond hair away from her face. Unable to contain her pent-up energy any longer, she rose to her feet and started pacing. "God, I've never felt so alive in my life." Her blue eyes glowed with excitement.

Ackerman chuckled softly. "That's nothing, darling. In a few hours the real fun begins."

"I can hardly wait."

For two years Connie Manley had prowled the underground labyrinth of Monroe College. She knew every inch of the tunnels. Her small size, often a liability in the world of sunshine, was an asset in the damp, dark world beneath the campus. She could move quickly through the tunnels, not having to worry about the low-hanging steam pipes and tight squeezes. She couldn't wait to get her prey on her turf.

"Herbert?" Ackerman said into the phone.

"Yes."

"Everything went flawlessly. Paul Moore has the bag."

"Excellent. They should be arriving within the next hour. Is everything in place?"

"Of course. Have I ever let you down?"

"Where are you calling from?" Queensbury asked.

"My office."

"Are you alone?"

"No, Connie Manley's here."

"Send her away."

Ackerman placed his hand over the mouthpiece of the phone. "Connie, it's time for you to get below." She nodded her head and silently left the professor's office. "She's gone."

"Have you made the arrangements for the players?"

"The same as the last time, Herbert. As soon as the game's over, they'll all be dead."

JACK GRIMALDI HAD to stay with the plane. The front landing gear had been damaged when the Saberliner slid off the runway. It was repairable, and the Air Force mechanic assigned to the airstrip appeared to know what he was doing, but Grimaldi wanted to be there to supervise.

Able Team and Dr. Stein crammed their way into Paul Moore's Bronco for the short trip to the Monroe College campus. Moore had stopped at a convenience store and phoned his office. When they arrived at the old power plant, three campus security guards were waiting.

"Did you get the stuff I wanted?"

"Yeah," Johnny Johnson said as he opened his truck. "I had a heck of a time finding tranquilizer guns. I could only come up with one."

"We still have the one that was dropped outside the window. That makes two."

"Did you get the blowpipes?" Lyons ask, barging into the conversation.

"Yeah," Johnson answered, eyeing Lyons with suspicion. "Why do you guys need this stuff?"

"Queensbury left the bag for us to find," Moore answered. "Everything in it is nonlethal. He was establishing the rules of the game. Whoever's down there won't be armed."

"Down there?"

"In the tunnels," Moore said as he reached for one of the two tranquilizer guns.

"Probably kids," Lyons said as he handed the other gun to Gadgets. "Pol and I will use the blowpipes."

"Sure, why not?" Pol said as he reached for a hollow tube. "If it's good enough for the President, it should be good enough for a bunch of kids."

"The President?" Nan asked, a puzzled look on her face.

Gadgets grinned at her. "We had a bet with the Secret Service a while back that we could assassinate the President if we wanted to. Pol hit him square in the middle of the forehead with a paint pellet fired from one of these."

"Yeah," Pol said with a laugh. "Fortunately for Ironman the Secret Service lacked my marksmanship skills."

Lyons snorted as he remembered how close he had come to being killed by "friendly" fire. Brognola had made a wager with an old buddy at the Service. If Able Team could "hit" the President, they would get a new gym for Stony Man. If not, the funds would go to spiff up the Secret Service facilities in Beltsville. On the way back from Stony Man the Secret Service man had been involved in a serious auto accident that had left him in a coma. None of the men actually protecting the President knew the attack was only a game—they took it seriously. Very seriously. A bullet had missed Ironman by less than an inch.

"I almost got my head blown off," Lyons growled under his breath.

"A small price to pay for a new gym."

Ironman glared at Pol but refused to rise to the bait. He had other things to worry about. "We'll have to rely on these as much as possible. We'll carry handguns only, but try to avoid using them."

Lyons looked at Moore, who nodded his head, his face grim. Both men had made another trip into the tunnels years earlier. Neither looked forward to the return engagement. The sun was up and the weather was quickly improving. The temperature was still dropping, but the front had moved through and the snow had tapered off to flurries. Nearly three inches of the white stuff was already on the ground.

"I hear it's going to be eighty today in L.A.," Pol said as he wiped his nose.

"You'll be a lot warmer than that in a few minutes," Lyons said as he fished a flashlight out of the trunk of the campus security car.

"What do you mean?"

"The new power plant uses some of the same pipe network. The tunnels have steam pipes that connect all the buildings on campus," Moore said as he took off his coat and pulled on a pair of coveralls. "The temperature can top a hundred degrees in some places."

"Then," Lyons said, "you turn a corner and get hit with a blast of cold air. It's like walking into a wall."

"Sounds like just what my cold needs," Pol said, sliding a foot into his coveralls.

"Where's my gear?" Nan asked.

"You don't get any," Lyons said flatly. "You're not going in."

"Now wait a minute!" Stein protested. "I didn't come all this way to be left out in the cold."

"Remember," Lyons said, his cold blue eyes focused on the scientist, "I didn't want you to come at all."

Gadgets gently pulled Nan away from Ironman. "He's right. There's no telling what we'll run into down there."

The scientist's eyes flashed with anger. "You, too?"

"Sorry."

"If I had my way," Pol said as he hooked his arm around Nan's waist, "I'd let you go."

She shot Blancanales a "drop dead" look and turned her attention back to Lyons. "What am I supposed to do while you're gone?"

"Wait."

CONNIE MANLEY STOPPED at an intersection and turned off her flashlight. The darkness was total. A short whistle escaped from her lips. The sound reverberated off the concrete walls and echoed into the darkness. From the corridor ahead there were two flashes of light. She answered by blinking her flashlight three times.

"Hi, Connie," said a voice from less than three feet away. Even with her experience and knowledge of the tunnels she hadn't seen Mike Chin. He had pressed himself into a narrow depression in the wall; unless her light had happened to fall across him, she would have walked by without seeing him.

He leveled his tranquilizer gun at her. "Bang, bang, you're dead."

"Excellent, Mike. Excellent! How did you rig the light?"

"Radio-controlled." Chin held up a palm-sized transmitter for Manley to see.

"Is everything ready?"

"Yeah. We have the trip wires set and the door's rigged as instructed."

"What about the signs?"

"They're all up."

"I'd say we're ready," Manley said with a smile.

"Let the games begin," Chin answered. "Let the games begin."

10

Gadgets had a blue nylon bag, about the size of a gym bag, slung over his left shoulder. He took up the rear as the four men moved down the steps toward the basement of the old power station.

"Look at this," Lyons said, pausing on the landing. There were drops of water on the stairs.

Moore bent and examined one of the puddles. "Probably melted snow. Someone's been here recently."

"Leads right to the entrance of the tunnels," Lyons said, pointing to a closed door barely visible at the end of a dark corridor.

"Do you think we should split up, Ironman?" Pol asked.

"No, it's too easy to get lost in there. Besides, this is the most direct route to the room."

"What room?" Pol asked as he fumbled inside his coveralls for a tissue.

"The room where we found the bodies the last time. It's about a quarter of a mile from here."

"Didn't even show on the original plans," Moore added. "For all we know Queensbury may have built it himself."

The four men moved rapidly toward the door leading to the tunnels. Lyons pulled up short when he saw a handwritten sign on the door: Beware! Danger Lurks Ahead! Turn Back Now Before It Is Too Late!

"Looks like a real fun bunch, Ironman," Blancanales said.

Lyons didn't answer; he was too busy checking the door to see if it had been rigged. He tested the doorknob; it was unlocked. Slowly he began to open the door. He felt a slight resistance when the door was about four inches open. Snaking his hand inside, Ironman felt the wire that had been tied to the inside knob. It was taut.

"Gadgets," Lyons said as he closed the door an inch to take the pressure off the trip wire, "see what you can do. Everyone else fall back."

The men retreated to the landing and took shelter in the stairwell. Gadgets reached inside his nylon bag and found a pair of wire cutters. Carefully he reached inside and snipped the wire. As soon as he felt the wire give, he slammed the door and dived to the left. With his back pressed against the concrete wall, he covered his face and eyes. Nothing happened.

"I guess I got it!" Gadgets shouted as he rose to his feet.

Before anyone could answer there was a rumble and a bright flash from behind the door.

"Then again," Pol said with a smile, "maybe you didn't."

"Thirty-second delay," Gadgets answered. "This guy's a real pain."

"That's a warning shot," Lyons said. "Queensbury just wanted to get our attention."

"Well," Gadgets answered, "he's certainly got mine. We'll have to take it slowly."

Lyons checked his watch and shook his head. "We don't have time. The toxin will be released in twenty-seven hours."

CONNIE MANLEY and Mike Chin were just about at the room when they heard the distant rumble of explosives.

"They're here," Chin said, mimicking the little girl from the movie *Poltergeist*.

"We better take up our positions. They'll head directly here."

Chin checked his dart gun for the tenth time. "I wish these things could fire more than once without reloading."

"We have the advantage," Manley answered as she rubbed black grease paint on her face. "We know the tunnels and they don't. We do it as planned. Hit-and-run guerrilla warfare."

Manley handed Chin the tube of grease paint. His hands were shaking. "You okay?" she asked.

"A little nervous," he confessed. "What if they start shooting real bullets at us?"

"Then we go to plan B."

A puzzled look covered Chin's face. "What's plan B?"

"If they start shooting, we get the hell out of here."

Chin nodded. He was looking forward to playing a real-live game of cat and mouse with campus security. He had spent nearly six weeks prowling the underground tunnels searching for the perfect ambush sites. His first attack point was near a four-way intersection of tunnels halfway between the room and the old power station. He could conceal himself behind a concrete support, fire a dart and disappear down the narrow corridor leading to the room. Less than a hundred feet down the tunnel was another support. Chin figured he would be able to fire at least six darts before security reached the room. He gathered up his weapons and placed them in a brown grocery bag. "Where will you be?"

Manley smiled like a Cheshire cat. "The last place anyone would expect me."

GADGETS REACHED into his bag and brought out a hand-held light about the size and shape of a loaf of bread. He turned the oversize monster on, but nothing happened.

"What's that?" Moore asked.

"An infrared lamp," Schwarz answered, pulling on the headgear he had used the day before to track Ironman. "Even this won't work in total darkness. It requires some light. Here, take a look."

Moore accepted the second unit and gave it a skeptical look. Without slipping the straps over his head, he held the viewing area up to his face. "I'll be damned!" he exclaimed.

While the beams of their flashlights could only penetrate the darkness for a distance of about twenty yards, Moore could see at least three hundred yards down the tunnel with the night glasses. And instead of just a narrow cone of light, every nook and cranny of the passageway was visible.

"This lantern," Gadgets began as he adjusted his headgear, "gives off the equivalent light of two dozen hundred-watt bulbs. If this were white light, it would be so bright that we'd need sunglasses."

"How many of these things do you have?"

"Just two. Do you want the second one?"

Moore was tempted. Instead, he handed the unit to Pol. "Lyons and I have been through these tunnels before and you guys haven't."

Lyons nodded. "Gadgets, you take the point. Pol, you take the rear."

Blancanales stopped just as he was about to pull the night vision unit on. "Hey, Gadgets, what happens if I sneeze in this thing?"

"Ten thousand volts will go up your nose."

"Great," Pol answered. "Maybe that'll clean out my sinuses."

"There's one thing you need to watch out for," Moore said. "All of the steam pipes have pressure release valves. If you hear a hissing sound, duck."

"This is getting to be more fun by the minute," Pol said as he adjusted the headgear.

MIKE CHIN'S FACE glistened with sweat from the intense heat of the overhead steam pipes as he pressed his back against the concrete support. He had played this game a thousand times in his head. He had considered every possibility and every possible direction of attack. He was ready. Or so he thought. When he heard muffled voices approaching, he smiled. "Showtime," he muttered under his breath.

In the distance there were three bobbing flashlights approaching. Chin placed the first dart in the firing chamber. Slowly he slid down the wall. He was confident he couldn't be seen. His only concern was that he would be heard. When he reached a kneeling position, he braced his arm against the concrete support and aimed at the center of the three flashlights. The lights were just over a hundred yards away and they hadn't broken their stride. Chin knew when he would fire. Fifty feet from his position the tunnel narrowed to a width of only four feet. The enemy would have to come through the opening one at a time.

"YOU SEE HIM?" Gadgets whispered to Pol.

"Yeah," he said as he moved up to the point with Gadgets. "See anyone else?"

"Not yet."

"You think he knows we've spotted him?"

"No," Gadgets answered, handing the infrared lantern to Ironman. "We'll move ahead and neutralize the target. If you see anything, whistle."

"Right," Ironman said as he accepted the lantern.

Gadgets and Pol, running in a crouched position, moved thirty feet ahead of the other two. Gadgets motioned to Pol that he would take the left side of the tunnel and that Blancanales should take the right side. Pol nodded.

At the point where the tunnel narrowed Gadgets and Pol stopped. A puddle of water, at least an inch deep, formed a miniature lake in the passage. It was impossible to avoid. If they attempted to jump the water, they would be heard by the sniper. If they walked through, they would also be heard.

Still unnoticed, both men were relieved to see that their target was armed with only a tranquilizer gun. Gadgets tucked his Beretta 93-R back inside his coveralls and brought out the awkward tranquilizer gun. He wished he'd had the opportunity to test-fire the weapon. He had no idea how accurate it was.

Carefully he lined up the sniper in his sights. But before he could fire Schwarz was distracted by a hissing sound directly above his head. He was hit with an unexpected blast of steam. The headgear absorbed most of the heat, but not all of it. The area between his hairline and the collar of the coveralls had turned the color of a freshly boiled Maine lobster. The shock caused Gadgets to lose his grip on his weapon, and it clattered to the floor.

"What the hell?" Chin shouted, rising to his feet.

"Freeze, turkey," Pol said, bringing the blowpipe to his lips.

Chin fired blindly in the general direction of the narrow passage. The dart bounced harmlessly off the wall and landed in the pool of water. Blancanales puffed his cheeks, and the dart exploded from the end of the three-foot-long tube. Chin, sensing the danger, dived to the right. Pol's dart ripped Chin's pant leg but failed to make contact with any skin. The student grabbed his bag and retreated before Pol could get another dart loaded into the pipe. "You okay?" he asked Gadgets.

"Fine," Schwarz answered as he ripped the headgear off. "The steam fogged up the lens in this thing. Looks like it's up to you."

Pol splashed through the puddle and followed Chin down the corridor. The Able Team Warrior slowed his pace and pressed his back against the wall. He was far enough away from the infrared lantern that the night vision glasses were losing their effectiveness. Pol also had a more immediate problem. He heard the sounds of men running from behind him but not in front. The sniper had stopped. Their early advantage of surprise had disappeared in a cloud of steam. Now the sniper knew where Pol was, but Blancanales had no idea about his opponent's position.

Then there was movement in the shadows up ahead. Pol tried to guess the sniper's next move, but the dart missed by nearly three feet. Something metallic-sounding rolled on the concrete a few feet in front of him, and Pol instantly recognized the shape. It was a stun grenade.

11

The world was moving in slow motion for Rosario Blancanales. He knew the flash from the grenade would blind everyone in the tunnel and allow the sniper to escape. There was no time to think, only time to react.

Pol leaped in the direction of the stun grenade, but the night vision glasses had affected his depth perception and he nearly dived over it. Placing his hands over his ears and closing his eyes, he tried to adjust the position of the grenade by crawling backward. He knew his Kevlar vest would stand a better chance of protecting him if he was centered over the explosive.

The force of the exploding grenade lifted Pol six inches off the ground. The percussion, while loud in the enclosed tunnels, was bearable for the rest of Able Team. Fortunately the rubber housing of the grenade kept any fragments from ripping him apart.

Totally disoriented, Blancanales rolled onto his back. The front of his white coveralls was scorched and still smoking. The Kevlar vest that had saved his

life so many times before had done the job again.
Gadgets was the first to arrive.

"You okay?" Concern was obvious in Schwarz's
voice.

Pol couldn't answer. He felt like a marionette with
tangled strings. When he tried to move his right
hand, it was the left that responded. His foot
twitched when he tried to speak.

"Is he all right?" Lyons asked as he and Moore
caught up.

"Won't be able to tell for a few minutes," Gadgets answered.

"You stay here. We'll go after the sniper."

"Right," Gadgets answered as he licked his finger and placed it on a spot on Pol's coveralls that was
still smoldering. The cloth hissed. "Idiot," Gadgets
muttered.

Moore and Ironman charged ahead. Fifty yards
from the spot where Pol had thrown his body on the
grenade they came to an intersection of tunnels. The
two men slowed to a stop.

"Which way?" Moore asked.

Lyons motioned to the left in the direction of the
room. "Turn off your light," he ordered. "I've got
an idea."

MIKE CHIN WAS TERRIFIED. He had never expected
the security guard to throw himself on a live grenade. He had never expected them to be wearing
night vision glasses. These guys were playing for

keeps. Chin had the sinking feeling that there was more to this than just a campus prank. He had heard the stories. Hell, legends, about the tunnels and what had happened in the seventies. Professor Ackerman had explained it so clearly how the press had over-reacted. He had been there, so he should know. But now Chin wasn't so sure.

He could make a run for one of the exits, but the closest one in this direction was nearly a quarter of a mile away. And then he saw the approaching glare of two flashlights.

"Come on out. We know you're there."

Chin was tempted to give it up, but something held him back. He knew the campus rules. Anyone caught in the tunnels would be expelled. How could he face his father if he got kicked out of college over a prank? No, he would have to try to make it to the exit.

"Come on, kid. Give it up," one of the men shouted. "I know you're planning on using the Spencer Hall exit and I've already got a guard posted there."

Chin's hands were shaking. The men following him knew the tunnel. There were only two ways out from his present location. One was past the men chasing him and the other was at Spencer Hall. He was trapped. He had to take out the two men following him. If he could get past them, no one would ever catch him.

Chin slid down the wall into a seated position. Steadying his elbows on his knees, he aimed the dart gun a few inches above the light on the left. Taking a deep breath and holding it, he squeezed the trigger. A moment later he heard the dart skipping on the concrete floor.

"There, Ironman." Chin was trapped in the circle of a beam of light. Before he could get up to run he felt a pair of strong hands yanking him to his feet.

"Game's over, Junior," Lyons snarled as he slammed the student against the wall. Moore had been a decoy. Lyons had stayed ten yards ahead while the security guard walked down the middle of the tunnel with the two lights held out at arm's length. Chin had assumed that there was a person behind each light. He had assumed incorrectly.

"Don't hit me," Chin said with tears running down his cheeks. "God, please don't hit me."

"I'll do a damn sight more than that if you don't do some quick talking," Lyons growled. "How many others are down here?"

Chin hesitated. Ironman slammed him against the wall hard enough to knock the wind from the frightened boy's lungs.

"Hey," Chin wailed, "you can't do this. I have rights."

Lyons lifted Chin a few inches off the ground until they were eye to eye. "Okay, punk," he hissed through clenched teeth, "you have the right to remain silent. Permanently."

"I know a place here in the tunnels, Carl," Moore said, holding his flashlight inches from Chin's eyes. "We could kill him and no one would ever find the body."

"Wait," Chin shouted as he fought back his tears. "There's only one other person down here."

"Where is he?" Lyons asked.

"She. Connie Manley."

"Where is *she*?"

"I don't know."

Lyons bounced Chin off the wall again. "I'm losing my patience. Where is she?"

"I don't know." The tears flowed from Chin's eyes. "If I knew, I'd tell you. You have to believe me."

"What do you know about Herbert Queensbury?"

"Nothing."

"Then who's your local contact?"

"I don't know what you mean."

"Someone sent you down here. Who was it?"

Before Chin could answer the tunnel echoed with the reverberation of high-powered ammunition. Chin's head exploded like a ripe melon.

Lyons and Moore doused their lights and dived for cover.

"Did you see a muzzle-flash?" Lyons whispered.

"No," Moore answered. "I don't even know which direction the bullet came from."

POL HAD RECOVERED enough to walk, but his balance was still suspect. "I feel drunk," he said as he leaned on Gadgets for support.

"You took a pretty good jolt."

"No shit, Sherlock," Pol said, rolling his neck. "You sure you know the way? I'd hate to get lost down here."

"Moore said to go to the next intersection and turn left—" Gadgets was interrupted by the sound of a shot being fired.

Blancanales and Schwarz jumped in opposite directions while reaching for their guns. Pol brought out his Uzi machine pistol from inside his coveralls. Gadgets had his Beretta 93-R cocked and ready.

"I'm still not hearing very well, but I'm pretty sure that wasn't an air pistol."

"That was a big boomer. At least a 7.62 mm." Gadgets reached for his communicator and hit the button. "Ironman, we heard a shot."

"Where are you?" Lyons answered instantly.

"Not sure. Near the intersection, I think."

"Good. I think we've got the sniper bracketed. Is your fancy headgear operational?"

"Negative. Mine's still fogged and the one Pol was wearing when the grenade went off is beyond repair."

"Proceed with caution. Somebody just raised the stakes."

"We're heading toward you now," Gadgets said.

"Shh," Pol hissed. "Listen."

In the distance they heard the sound of running feet and labored breathing. Whoever was running had assumed that all of the men had already passed his position and didn't realize he was running straight toward Pol and Schwarz.

"Freeze!" Pol shouted.

The heavyset man was blowing hard from his sprint down the corridor. At the sound of Pol's voice he dropped his flashlight, brought his M-21 to his waist and kicked the customized sniper rifle onto autoburn. The 20-round clip, minus the bullet that had killed Mike Chin, erupted in a hail of death. Chunks of concrete exploded as the 190-grain Sako Super Match cooked out of the barrel at nearly twenty-eight hundred feet per second. Several of the heavy slugs penetrated low-hanging pipes, causing them to release a spray of scalding steam.

Pol and Schwarz were safely tucked behind concrete supports and the bullets from the M-21 didn't find them. The steam was another matter. The temperature in the tunnel immediately rose from hot to unbearable.

Before the sniper could ram another clip into his hungry weapon, Gadgets rolled from his position of safety and fired a 3-round burst from his Beretta. The first shot was wide to the right, but the next two found their mark. Both bullets hit the sniper in the middle of the chest. They rattled around inside until his heart and lungs were reduced to hamburger.

Pol and Schwarz approached the dead man cautiously. The M-21 lay on the ground next to the corpse. Perched on top of the weapon was a NATO-standard infrared night vision sight.

"Serious weapon," Pol said, giving it a kick. He was sure the man wasn't playing "possum," but he knew better than to take any chances.

The gunfire had brought Lyons and Moore on a dead run. "You two okay?" Ironman asked as he held the flashlight on the face of the corpse. He had hoped it would be Queensbury, but it wasn't.

"We're fine," Schwarz answered.

"You know this guy?" Lyons asked Moore.

"Yeah, he's a professor, a real nut case. His name's Dan Ackerman. Probably Queensbury's inside man. We suspected he was involved with the first incident but could never prove it." The head of security surveyed the damage from the ruptured pipe and shook his head. There was nearly an inch of boiling water on the floor tunnel. The pipes were no longer hissing. The big boiler at the new power plant had lost its pressure.

"Shit, what a mess. First snow of the year and there won't be a building on campus with any heat." Moore pulled a walkie-talkie from his belt and began explaining the situation to the men up top. Not only would they need a maintenance crew, they were going to need the local cops and the coroner.

"By the way," Pol said cheerfully, "this steam's great. It's the first time I've been able to breathe in a week."

"Some cold," Gadgets said with a mischievous smile. "Had to sit on a grenade to get rid of it."

Lyons waited until Moore was finished talking to his people aboveground. "What do you know about Connie Manley?"

Moore shrugged. He returned his walkie-talkie to his belt. "Never heard of her."

"Who's Connie Manley?" Pol asked.

Ironman's face was sterner than usual. "She's the person waiting for us somewhere in these tunnels."

12

Connie Manley's nostrils had flared as she'd watched the tall man slam Mike Chin against the wall. From her hiding place above a row of water pipes she had been too far away to hear what was being said.

"Bastards," she'd muttered to herself. She had known Chin would be too weak to resist even the mildest interrogation. It would only be a matter of time before he told them about her. She was glad she hadn't revealed her hiding place to the weakling.

Manley had flinched at the sound of gunfire. She'd watched in horror as Mike Chin's body had jerked, then crumpled to the floor. It had taken all of her willpower to keep from screaming. And then the men who had captured Mike had quickly turned off their flashlights. The tunnel had become as dark and quiet as a crypt. There were no more shots.

Connie Manley's mind searched for answers. Why had they shot Mike? Why had they turned off their lights? What the hell was going on?

In the darkness she heard muffled voices; they were too faint to make out any of the words, but she knew the men had left. Manley waited a few more minutes before jumping softly down from her hiding place.

She held her position in the darkness and cocked her head. In the two years since her first visit to the tunnels she had spent many hours in their total darkness. During that time she had developed acute hearing. In the distance there was an explosion and more gunfire. What the hell was going on? she wondered to herself in the black emptiness.

Slowly, feeling her way along the tunnel wall, she made her way toward Chin's body. When she sensed that she was close, she used her body as a shield and flipped on her penlight. The tiny bulb seemed incredibly bright to her dilated eyes. A few feet away lay Mike Chin. At least what was left of him. The 7.62 mm round had entered his head just above the right ear. The entire left side of the student's face and head was red goo.

Manley felt her anger growing. Her breath came in short gulps. Professor Ackerman had warned her that the campus pigs might shoot first and ask questions later. That was why she had brought along something better than the dart gun. Reaching into the rear pocket of her jeans, she pulled out the chrome .380 automatic. She fed a round into the firing chamber. In the knapsack slung over her shoulder she found one of the flash grenades Ackerman had given her. Pulling the pin, she threw it as far as she could down the tunnel. Crouching with her back toward the grenade, she covered her ears and closed her eyes. Only two hundred feet from the grenade when it erupted, she was thrown forward but wasn't stunned.

Shaking off the effects of the percussion, she jumped to her feet. "Come and get me, you bastards!" she shouted into the gloom. "I'm waiting for you!"

BEFORE LYONS COULD FINISH telling Moore to have security stall the police who had just arrived, he found himself knocked face first to the floor by the percussion of a stun grenade. The explosion was far enough down the corridor that it had lost most of its force by the time it reached their position. But it did manage to get everyone's attention.

They all heard her taunting challenge.

"What were you saying about going into hiding, Ironman?" Pol asked, shaking his head to reorient himself.

Lyons ignored the barb from Blancanales. "We'll move ten yards at a time. The lead man will provide cover as the last man moves up to the point."

"What weapon should we use?" Gadgets asked. "The dart gun or our handguns?"

"Take no chances," Lyons said sternly as he tucked his dart gun into his belt. "The lead man will be a sitting duck. We'll probably have to concede Manley the first shot. Let's not give her two. We'll have to cover roughly three hundred yards. There are no obstructions on the floor, but there are some low-hanging pipes. Keep your head down.''

"Good luck," Moore said as Pol plunged head-long into the darkness.

The Able Team warrior's foot slipped on a wet spot on the floor and, in his crouched position, he nearly lost his balance. He scrambled to the left side of the tunnel, pressed his back to the cold stone and strained his ears for any sound. Holding his dark flashlight at arm's length, he hit the button and examined the terrain ahead. Seeing no barriers, he gave one short whistle and turned his light off. In the dark silence he felt Gadgets slide by and take up the point. Schwartz's light flicked on, then off, and was followed by a short whistle. Pol felt Ironman move by and take the lead.

They had played their dangerous game of leapfrog six times already with no sign of Manley. Ironman's light flashed three times. Low pipes.

The heat and darkness dredged up memories that Blancanales would just as soon forget—the nights he had spent on deep-penetration missions in Vietnam. He had made many HALO jumps on moonless nights in suspected VC areas. He would go in, raise a little hell, then make his way back home as best he could.

Blancanales moved low and fast past Gadgets, who was pressed against the right side of the tunnel. He jagged to the left as he passed Ironman, then moved under the first set of low pipes.

The moment Pol flipped on his light a shot rang out from overhead. A .380 slug slammed into the center of his chest but was easily stopped by his Kevlar vest. Pol dropped the light and dived for the cover of darkness. "She's in the overhead pipes!" he shouted.

"I know," Lyons answered, "but I don't have a good angle."

Both men froze as they heard something clatter to the floor.

"Grenade!" Pol yelled as he tried to cover his eyes and ears. Lyons rolled into a tight ball, turning his back toward the grenade. It erupted in a brilliant flash, knocking both Lyons and Blancanales face first onto the concrete floor.

Manley jumped silently from the overhead pipe and removed the padding she had shoved into her ears. She moved toward Ironman and flashed a light in his face. Lyons felt as if he were encased in six feet of petroleum jelly. Setting her light on the floor, Manley grabbed him by the hair and shoved her .380 automatic under his nose. Lyons was unable to resist.

"You don't look so tough now, big boy," she hissed.

Between the light in his face and the effects of the stun grenade, Ironman's eyes had trouble focusing on the gun. But he knew it was there. He also knew that his number was up.

Slowly Manley pulled the hammer back. "This is for what you did to Mike Chin."

Just as she pulled the trigger, Manley was hit broadside by Gadgets. The round from her automatic skipped harmlessly into the darkness as the blast echoed throughout the subterranean complex.

Gadgets, being the farthest away when the stun grenade had exploded, had been the first to recover. He was too unsteady to risk a shot; he knew that he might hit Ironman. His only option was hand-to-hand combat.

The Able Team commando and Manley tumbled over her penlight, shattering the bulb. The tunnel was totally dark. In his weakened state Schwarz realized he had a tiger by the tail. Manley turned her claws toward his eyes, opening up four parallel gashes on his cheek.

"Let go of me, you bastard," she snarled, groping in the darkness for her gun.

"Calm down," Gadgets said as he tried to restrain the woman. "I don't want to hurt you."

"Just like you didn't want to hurt Mike Chin?" Manley brought her knee up to Schwarz's groin. In the darkness she missed dead center, but she was close enough to make him release his grip.

"Damn!" Gadgets groaned as Manley slithered away. He was able to grab her ankle before she completely disappeared. She kicked back with her free foot, catching Gadgets on the top of the head. "I've had about enough of this," he muttered. With one catlike leap he was on top of the smaller woman, pinning her to the floor.

Gadgets felt something metallic being shoved under his Kevlar vest. Manley had located her gun. With all of his strength, he grabbed Manley's hand and tried to twist the gun away from her.

Lyons, fighting off the effects of the stun grenade, struggled to his feet. His legs couldn't bear his weight and he tumbled forward, banging his head on a low-hanging pipe. He landed on all fours. He knew Gadgets was in trouble, but he was unable to help. Pol, who had been battered twice by grenades, was unconscious. Gadgets was on his own.

The chrome automatic erupted six times until it finally clicked empty.

"No!" Lyons shouted. With seconds seeming like hours, Ironman frantically searched the darkness for a flashlight. Pol groaned off to one side. Lyons scrambled in his direction. Blancanales was just starting to reorient himself when Lyons touched his chest. Pol tried to reach for his Uzi pistol, but Ironman clamped a strong hand on his wrist. "It's me," he said softly. "Where's your light?"

"Here."

Lyons accepted the flashlight, flipped it on and rolled it across the floor. If Connie Manley was still on the prowl, holding the light would be an invitation to a funeral. His own.

With his eyes completely dilated, the meager light was enough to make the tunnel seem as if it were bathed in bright sunlight. Twenty feet away Gadgets was lying on top of Connie Manley.

Neither one was moving.

13

Carl Lyons picked up the flashlight and inched his way toward the tangled duo of Schwarz and Manley. Gadgets lay on top of the smaller woman; the .380 automatic was next to them. The floor was crimson. Gadgets groaned and moved slightly, and Ironman pulled the two apart. They had each taken three of the six rounds in the chest. Schwarz's Kevlar vest had stopped the bullets but, fired from such close range, it hadn't absorbed the full impact. Gadgets was going to have some nasty bruises.

Connie Manley wasn't as lucky; she hadn't been wearing a vest.

Her eyes were wide open, but they could no longer see. Two of the bullets had hit her in the stomach, the other just below the sternum. The low-powered slugs had been just as fatal as three rounds from a .44 Magnum because of her small size.

"You okay, Gadgets?"

Schwarz nodded as he touched his sore ribs. "I feel as if I've been kicked by a mule. Where's Pol?"

"Right here, Homes," Blancanales said as he pulled off Schwarz's vest and examined his injuries. "Looks like a couple of cracked ribs." Pol reached for his first-aid bag. "I'll tape you up."

Gadgets gritted his teeth and held his arms out of the way as Blancanales wrapped several layers of tape around the damaged area. "Hey, man, that's too tight. I still have to breathe," he said, grimacing with pain. "This doesn't seem fair."

"What's that?" Pol asked as he tore off another strip of the white tape before putting the roll back into his bag.

"You fall on a grenade and nothing happens. I take a few rounds in the vest from a peashooter and I can't inhale without seeing stars."

"Next grenade's all yours."

"Thanks." Gadgets gingerly put his vest back on, testing the limits of his mobility.

"You two ready?" Lyons asked.

"Yup," Pol said, reaching for both his and Gadgets's gear. "Lead the way, bwana."

"You think there's anyone else down here, Ironman?" Schwarz asked.

"Let's hope not, but we'll act as if there is."

It took three rounds of leapfrog to arrive at the room. Its original purpose was long-forgotten and it didn't appear on any of the maps the engineers had of the tunnels. The room had probably been a tool storage area during construction, but there was no one around who could confirm that. To Lyons, the room brought back bitter memories. He and Moore had spent two days in the tunnels, searching for the missing students. They had found them in this room. A group suicide.

The original wooden door had been replaced with a heavy metal fire door. The three locks that were supposed to seal the room had all been filed through and the doorknob was missing. With the slightest touch, Lyons knew the door would swing open. A hand-lettered sign had been taped at eye level: Danger! Enter at Your Own Risk!

"What do you think, Ironman?" Pol asked.

"It's a trap," Lyons answered without hesitation.

"This appears to be the only door," Pol said, scratching his head. "How do you propose to get inside?"

"We'll make another door." Ironman motioned for Gadgets to take over.

Schwarz pulled an eight-foot-long rope of plastic explosives from his rucksack. Working about three feet to the left of the door and starting near the floor, he formed a crude circle on the wall with the explosives. "Any idea how thick this wall is?" he asked, tapping it with a knuckle.

"It's cinder block," Lyons answered.

"This should do the trick, then," Gadgets said as he stuck a remote-controlled detonator into the flexible plastic. "You guys might want to back up."

Blancanales and Lyons retreated a few yards down the corridor and were soon joined by Schwarz. Gadgets extended the antenna on the palm-sized radio device, checked the position of his partners, then pushed the red button. The explosion was tame compared to that of the stun grenades. The flash was less than the average strobe of a 35 mm camera and the noise sounded like the backfiring of a truck. The tunnel quickly filled with a swirling white cloud of dust.

"Let's have a look," Gadgets said as he waved the smoke away. The explosive had done its job. A hole, large enough for Able Team to crawl through, had been opened in the wall. After moving some of the larger pieces of rubble, Lyons crawled belly down into the room. He was soon joined by Pol and Gadgets.

The space was about twelve feet square. In the middle of the floor was a low table, the kind found in Japanese restaurants. On the table stood two dozen candles, some of which had remained lit following the explosion. The room was cluttered with various items: books were on the floor; a ratty fishnet had been hung on the wall; fishing tackle and an exercise bike were in one corner.

Seated at the head of the table was a mannequin. The face had been removed from the dummy and a photograph of Herbert Queensbury had been attached.

"This is too weird," Pol whispered, as if concerned the mannequin could hear him.

"Gadgets, check the door."

"Holy shit," Gadgets said as he turned his light toward the door. "There's enough PE 4 explosives here to bring the entire roof down. If we had opened that door, they would have had to dig us out to bury us...if they could find any pieces big enough to bury."

Lyons slowly moved his light around the room, checking every corner and object for a possible booby trap.

"Hey, look," Pol said, using his light to point at the mannequin. "It's got a letter in its hand." Pol inched closer to the dummy and shone his light on the envelope. "The letter's addressed to you, Ironman."

"Don't touch it," Lyons said as he moved next to Pol. "Knowing Queensbury, it's probably rigged."

"How are we going to get it without touching it?" Gadgets asked.

"I'm not sure, but Queensbury always leaves the tools to solve the problem nearby." Ironman's light circled the room again. It stopped when it reached a fishing pole leaning against the wall. "Bingo. See if you can find something to attach to the letter."

"How about this?" Pol asked as he picked up a spring-loaded paper clip.

"Perfect," Lyons said, running out a few feet of twelve-pound test line. "You guys go on out and move well down the hall."

"You sure, Ironman?" Gadgets asked.

"Yeah, but promise me one thing."

"What's that?"

"If anything happens, you'll track down Queensbury."

Gadgets slapped Lyons on the back. "You got it, but I won't wear a tie to your funeral."

"Fair enough."

After his two partners had safely cleared the room, Lyons tied the heavy clip to the end of the fishing line. He pinched its mouth open and slid it over the end of the letter in the mannequin's hand. Running more line from the fishing rod, Lyons slid out of the hole in the wall. He carefully moved down the corridor, never allowing the line to lose its slack. "You guys ready?"

"Sure, why not?" Pol said as he knelt behind a concrete support.

Gadgets, who had wormed his way into a crevice, gave Ironman a thumbs-up.

Lyons took the slack out of the line. He extended his arms in the direction of the room, then jerked the pole backward as if he were setting the hook on a largemouth bass. He began reeling the line in as fast as he could. The letter danced out of the hole Gadgets had created and skipped across the floor toward Lyons.

The ground began to shake and a faint rumbling came from the direction of the room. A multicolored column of fire erupted out of the hole in the wall, and the steel door was blown from its hinges. The supports holding the ceiling buckled, and with a groan, tons of dirt collapsed into the tunnel.

Able Team was far enough from the room that they were only hit with noise and light.

"Man," Pol said, rubbing his eyes, "I don't know about you guys, but I haven't seen this many fireworks since the Fourth of July."

"The dummy must have been packed with explosives and a trip wire was connected to the letter," Gadgets said.

"Speaking of the letter," Pol said, "what does it say?"

Lyons tore open the envelope and peered inside. There was a note written on plain white paper.

Congratulations, Carl. You've earned the final clue as to where you may find me. Across from the Meadow, you'll find your goal. The Gamesmaster.

"What does that mean?" Pol asked after he read the message.

"Let's see," Gadgets answered, taking the note from Pol's hand. "It makes a poem. Almost heaven, where New is old. Across from the Meadow, you'll find your goal.''

"Robert Frost, he ain't," Pol said. "What do we do now?"

Lyons frowned. "We head back to the Farm and see if Bear can work some of his computer magic on this thing."

14

"Die, fascist!" The slogan was shouted as the next volley was launched.

The campus security guard ducked behind a tree to avoid the onslaught. He was outmanned and outflanked.

Paul Moore watched the scenario from the window of the old power station. The guard's only chance was to run while the enemy reloaded. Two steps from the safety of his car he was hit squarely in the side of the head.

"Nerds three, pigs nothing," taunted a skinny kid with long hair as he vanished into the woods.

Moore managed a slight smile as the campus cop brushed the snow from his hair. As he bent over to shake the rapidly melting white stuff from his collar, another snowball hit him just below the belt and squarely on the left cheek. Wiping the snow from his backside, he jumped into his car.

The lack of heat, the first snowfall of the season, and the strange rumbling sounds from underground had brought the students out in force. With few classes scheduled on Saturday, the trio of unusual events had been enough to trigger an impromptu snow carnival. On fraternity row snow forts had been built, then trashed by rival fraternities. The Sigma Chis had constructed a ten-foot-tall, anatomically accurate snowman. With a well-placed balloon the frat boys showed that they were proponents of "safe sex."

A crowd of over a hundred were milling around outside the old power plant. A half-dozen police cars, their blue lights flashing, had filled the parking lot. Reporters and gawkers had pulled off the access road and were parked on the snow-covered lawn. A technician from a Louisville television station was busy aiming the dish on top of the brightly painted van at some distant satellite.

"We have two known dead," Moore said as he turned from the window to face Walter Gordon, the university's president. And we don't have a report on the last explosion."

"Paul!" a breathless guard gasped as he entered the building. "The ground has collapsed in front of the chemistry building. There's a ten-foot-deep crater."

"What?" Walter Gordon exclaimed. Only in his early forties, Gordon had a full head of white hair that made him look at least ten years older. Three days a week in the gym, two miles a day in the campus pool, and regular visits to a tanning salon gave him a healthy glow. With degrees from Harvard and

Amherst, he was the prototype of the modern college president.

Nan Stein paced in a tight circle, kicking herself for allowing the men to enter the tunnel without her. She would rather be inside facing the danger than standing idly by dealing with the unknown.

"I hope they're all right," she said as she glanced for the thousandth time at the door leading to the tunnels.

Gordon ignored the woman; Paul Moore had his undivided attention. "You were here the last time this happened. I wasn't. How do we handle it?"

Moore shrugged. "Tell it like it is and don't try to be too cute. Everyone around here remembers Queensbury. Just play it straight up."

The vice provost of student affairs, a portly man in his late fifties, stuck his head in the door. "We've got some reporters out here who want a statement."

"How many?" Gordon asked.

"The local paper, the school paper and a Louisville television station."

"What do you think?" he asked, turning to Moore.

"It's your call. The FBI will be here within the hour and they'll put a gag on the whole thing."

Gordon rubbed his chin. He knows that his job was on the line and that if he left under a cloud, he might never find another college willing to hire him. The president of the college during Queensbury's first hit had been fired for trying to cover up the incident. He wasn't going to make the same mistake. "Bring them in."

The vice provost escorted the three reporters into the building. The local man, Cy Oats, was a burned-out journalist who had bounced steadily downward since his taste for martinis had cost him a staff position on the *Los Angeles Times*. At one time or another he had worked for all the major, and most of the minor, newspapers in the Midwest. He had the thin, drawn look of a heavy drinker. His skin was blotchy and his eyes were rimmed in red.

The television newsman looked as if he had just stepped from the pages of *Gentlemen's Quarterly*. Every hair was in place. A smile of well-capped teeth seemed permanently plastered between his chin and nose. In his right hand was a microphone that led to the cameraman, who was following twenty feet behind.

The reporter for the campus newspaper, Mark Strunk, was a stringy-haired throwback to the sixties. He was tall and thin and flashes of a bright tie-dyed shirt could be seen whenever his blue jean jacket flipped open.

The trio immediately began shouting questions. Gordon silenced them with one wave of his hand. "One at a time, please."

"There are rumors that at least ten people have been killed. Is that true?" the television reporter asked, getting his question in first.

Gordon looked at Moore for help, but the security chief shrugged and shoved his hands into his pockets. The president had opened this can of worms; campus security wasn't going to help him dig his way out.

"The rumors are unfounded. There have been two known fatalities," Gordon finally said.

"Three," Lyons said as he emerged from the tunnels. "And get them the hell out of here."

The glare of the klieg lights immediately shifted to the Able Team warrior. His eyes still dilated from the darkness of the tunnel, the big man from Stony Man shielded his face from the bright lights.

"Turn that thing off," he roared as he charged toward the camera. The cameraman was no fool. One look at Ironman was enough to convince him to follow orders. The light clicked off. The three reporters immediately began shouting questions and protests as Moore hustled them out of the room.

"Who are you?" Gordon demanded.

"I could ask you the same question," Lyons said, unzipping his coveralls.

"Where's Gadgets?" Nan interrupted, her voice ragged with panic.

"Gadgets and Pol will be here in a minute. They're talking to some policemen in the tunnel."

Stein clutched her heart and exhaled. "Thank heavens. When you said someone else was dead..." Her voice trailed off, and she headed toward the doorway to wait for the other men to return.

"What was the big explosion?" Moore asked.

"Queensbury had the room rigged."

"And the Manley girl?"

"Dead."

"You killed one of my students?" Gordon's eyes were wide with amazement. He stared at Lyons as if he were a giant bug that had just crawled out from under a flat rock.

Ironman had seen the look many times. The people who lived in secure little neighborhoods and only associated with the proper people never understood the world in which Able Team operated. Men like Walter Gordon, and most of the gnomes in Washington, only dealt with violence in the abstract. Over a glass of wine or imported mineral water the ruling elite thought they had all the answers. Lyons knew firsthand that when you stared down the barrel of a weapon you didn't have time for abstractions. You followed your instincts or you died.

"Yes," he finally answered, "I killed one of your students. The police in the tunnel have her gun and the twenty-odd pounds of explosives she was carrying."

"Oh." Gordon regained his composure before he continued. "I don't believe in physical violence," he said, adjusting his tie.

"Yeah," Lyons said, shaking his head. "Neither did that liberal columnist in Washington. It didn't stop him from shooting the kid who was skinny-dipping in his pool."

Gordon shook his head and walked away. He obviously thought it was useless to reason with some people.

Pol and Gadgets emerged from the tunnel in front of two men pushing a stretcher. The Able Team duo quickly ran into the power station before anyone could question them.

The sight of the stretcher triggered an uproar. Television cameras rolled. Questions were shouted from behind the yellow tape the police had strung around the building and parking lot. The media people, who had been waiting in the snow, demanded answers. The reporters stood a better chance of getting a comment from the body of Dan Ackerman than from the two men pushing the stretcher.

Mark Strunk, from the campus paper, brought his 35 mm camera up to his eye and snapped a half-dozen shots of the body being loaded into the ambulance. Before the rear door was closed, the men of Able Team emerged from the building.

Strunk's motor drive advanced the film as quickly as the reporter could hit the shutter. He adjusted the zoom lens to the maximum length and focused in on the face of Carl Lyons. Queensbury had requested as many shots as possible. He held the button down until the shutter refused to click again. Strunk checked the counter on the top of the camera; it read thirty-six.

The young man waited until the car with Lyons had pulled away before heading back to his dorm room. The snow was deep enough that some made its way into the college reporter's low-top sneakers. He ignored the clammy cold attacking his feet and trudged toward the four-story brownstone co-ed dormitory near the center of campus. The courtyard in front of the dorm was alive with activity, but Strunk was only interested in getting to his room. And the telephone.

He placed his camera on his desk and picked up the note from his roommate. He was relieved when he discovered his roommate and a group of friends had gone over to General Butler State Park in Kentucky to try their hand at skiing. It meant he wouldn't be disturbed.

Picking up the phone, he dialed the number he had committed to memory. He got an answer before the second ring.

"Yes?"

"This is Strunk."

"Hold on."

After a brief pause, he heard a familiar voice—Herbert Queensbury. "Mark! How good to hear from you. I had really expected to hear from Connie."

Strunk tried to control his emotions, but it was a losing battle. "Connie's dead. So are Ackerman and Chin."

"What went wrong?" Queensbury asked softly.

"I don't know. Before I could find out any details, he threw everyone from the press out."

"He?"

"The big blond guy you told me about. Lyons."

"He's there?"

"He was. He just left."

"Did he kill the others?"

"Probably. There have been some big explosions all over campus this morning."

"Find out what you can," Queensbury said abruptly. "Call me back when you have more information."

"Right."

HERBERT QUEENSBURY returned the phone to its cradle and rubbed his hands together in anticipation. "Lyons, my friend. You haven't disappointed me yet."

"What was that?" Alfred Potts asked as he looked up from his computer terminal.

"They have the second half of the clue. They should be here in a matter of hours."

Potts shook his head and stared at his screen. He was more concerned with his present problem. "I think they're onto us."

"Oh?"

"Yes. I'm still shadowing the access of the Stony Man computers, but they're calling up information that makes no sense."

Queensbury frowned and swiveled the monitor in his direction. "Let me have a look." He scrolled through the most recent information. "Shut it down. Now!"

"Right," Potts answered. His fingers raced across the keyboard. The monitor went blank. "We're disconnected."

"This game's getting better and better. Their computer man tried to bury us with information while attempting to track us down. Excellent."

"Should I send them our little present?"

Queensbury's mouth lifted slightly at the corners into a menacing, sarcastic smile. "By all means, send them our gift."

15

"Got it," Aaron Kurtzman said into the telephone as he finished typing the second part of the clue into his computer system. "I don't know what it means, but I've got it."

Lyons glanced over at Jack Grimaldi. "How long before we get back to the farm?"

"We're going to have to jump over a weather front," he replied as he checked the Saberliner's flight path. "We should be there in about an hour."

Ironman nodded. "We'll be home in an hour, Bear," Lyons said.

"Right. Brognola will be back from Washington by then. Oh, by the way, Queensbury quit tapping into our computer."

"Good. How much damage was done?"

"Hard to say. Everything will be scrambled till I discover how he broke in."

"It takes a thief to catch a thief."

"Huh?"

"Maybe I should say it takes a hacker to catch a hacker."

"Oh, right. I'll get right on this clue and I'll try to have something for you when you hit the ground."

"Roger." Lyons returned the microphone to the hook on the front panel of the airplane and moved back to the passenger section.

Gadgets had his shirt off and Pol was retaping Schwarz's cracked ribs. Pol was taking his time and correcting the hurried job he'd done in the tunnel.

"How's that feel?" Blancanales asked.

"Fine, as long as I don't inhale or exhale."

"Air pollution's bad for you, anyway."

Nan Stein's eyes flashed with anger. "Don't you guys ever take anything seriously?"

Gadgets slipped a free arm around the woman's waist and pulled her close. "Only one thing."

"You're incorrigible," she said, pushing him away.

The jet hit an unexpected air pocket and dropped about thirty feet. Gadgets ended up in Nan's lap. Pol bumped his head on the ceiling of the cabin, and the contents of the first-aid kit scattered across the floor.

Nan grinned at the man in her lap. "You need to go on a diet."

"Sorry," Grimaldi said from the pilot's seat. "We're crossing over the storm front right now. It could be a little rough for the next few minutes. You might want to buckle up."

As Nan helped Gadgets to his feet, she glanced out the window. The swirling storm chased the smile from her lips, and she shivered.

"What's wrong?" Gadgets asked.

"This storm front is the perfect delivery system for my toxin."

"Explain," Lyons demanded.

"Dumping my toxin into any of these clouds, because of the size and power of the front, would be like putting it in a giant blender. The toxin would be stirred and spread over a huge area.

"How big an area?"

Nan looked out the window again. "An area roughly the size of Texas."

"Jack," Lyons shouted toward the front of the jet, "what's the weather forecast?"

"We should get some snow at the Farm tomorrow."

"Where's the front headed?"

"Up the East Coast."

"When will it hit New York?"

"Hey, do I look like the weather man?" Grimaldi protested.

"You follow the weather like a millionaire follows the stock market. Just give me your best guess."

Grimaldi smiled; he knew Lyons was right. He never knew when or where his services would be needed. Weather was the most important variable in flying, and Grimaldi didn't like surprises. "It'll probably hit midtown around midday tomorrow."

"Just about when our time runs out," Lyons said gravely.

AARON KURTZMAN USED his remote control to turn the volume up on the Phil Collins CD that was playing on his stereo. With the amount of time the Bear spent in his electronic cave, Brognola had complained only slightly when the requisition for the stereo system crossed his desk.

Queensbury was good. Very good. Twice Kurtzman thought he had tracked down the location of the Gamesmaster's computer center. Twice he had been wrong. Queensbury had been too smart to send the information directly to his own computer center. Instead, he'd downloaded all the pirated information through a series of computer bulletin boards spread from one end of the country to the other. Anyone with a modem and the proper entry code to the bulletin board had access to some of the most confidential information the government had on file. Bear erased the information from the data banks whenever he found it. For billing purposes many of the boards kept logs of who had called and when. Kurtzman cross-checked to see if any of the numbers appeared on the records of the other boards. Some of the numbers led to other bulletin boards, some to computer junkies. Each trail was a blind alley.

Kurtzman shook his head. He knew that if he could hack his way into other people's data bases, there was always the risk someone might find a way into his. Bear thought he knew all the tricks; Queensbury had taught him a few new ones.

Kurtzman glanced up from his screen when he heard Hal Brognola enter his lair.

"Status," Brognola barked.

"Damage control at this point. I'm backtracking, trying to locate Queensbury by his computer hookup. So far, nothing."

"What are your chances of finding him using that method?"

"Eventually I'll track him down," Bear said with more confidence than he felt.

"Give me a time frame."

"Two days minimum, unless I get lucky."

"We've got eighteen hours. Drop the search for Queensbury and concentrate on breaking the message."

"Right," Bear agreed. By the time he located the point where all the information had been dumped, Queensbury would likely be long gone.

"Give me the complete message," Brognola said.

"Almost heaven, where New is old. Across from the Meadow, you'll find your goal."

"Why are New and Meadow capitalized?"

"Um," Bear said, rubbing his chin, "maybe they're proper names?"

"And if they are?"

"Well, I can cross-reference the words against each other and do a full data search."

"Explain," Brognola said as he unwrapped a cigar.

"I can check everything we have on file and highlight any entry that has both the words *new* and *meadow*."

"How long will it take?"

"With my system?" Bear shook his head. "Unless I get lucky it might be better to follow the computer path back to Queensbury."

Brognola chewed on the end of his cigar. "Would anything help?"

"If I could get access to a Cray, I could have the information a lot quicker."

"A Cray. One of those super computers?"

"Yeah."

"Who has one?"

Bear pivoted in his chair, his fingers dancing across one of his keyboards. "I know the CIA has one and the Naval Institute— What the hell?" The Monitor Bear was using had suddenly blinked off. One by one all of the monitors in the room flicked off.

"What's going on?" Brognola demanded.

"That bastard."

"Who?"

"Queensbury. He planted a virus in my system."

"A virus?"

"Damn." Kurtzman slammed his fist on his desktop. "With the amount of raw data I've been running through the system in the past twenty-four hours, he must have snuck in a bug."

"Put all of this into English."

"I'm out of business till I find the bug and clean it out of my system."

16

The sun was down and so was the temperature when the Saberliner landed at Stony Man. The Siberian Express that had swept into the Midwest had been stalled by a large low pressure center in the Atlantic two hundred miles off Long Island. The center of the storm was hovering over the warm waters of the Great Lakes. Catching its breath and rebuilding its strength, the storm was nearly ready to deliver a knockout punch to the eastern seaboard. Buffalo already had seven inches of snow and six more were forecast by morning. Washington, Philadelphia, New York and Boston were all under a severe weather advisory. The snow was expected to reach Manhattan around noon the next day, two hours before the Gamesmaster's deadline.

"Wow. Ironman, look at this." Grimaldi pointed at the front window of the Saberliner.

Lyons peered out through the gloom toward the main hangar. Parked on the tarmac were two Sikorsky Black Hawk multirole helicopters. Both birds bore U.S. Army markings.

"Look at the armament on those babies," the pilot said with a hint of envy in his voice. "We could have some fun with those."

Lyons wasn't impressed. Modern weapons were merely the tools of the trade. A carpenter doesn't get excited about a new hammer.

Less than five minutes after Grimaldi had touched down, Able Team and Nan Stein were in the war room with Hal Brognola. The head Fed nodded at Nan—they both chose to forgo a formal introduction. The clock was ticking.

Lyons pulled up a chair and looked around. "Where's Bear?"

Brognola unwrapped a cigar and tossed the wrapper in the general direction of the wastebasket in the corner. "He flew up to Langley."

"Langley!" Ironman said with a stunned expression.

"What's he doing at CIA headquarters, boss?" Pol asked, falling heavily into a chair.

"Queensbury got into our computer system and completely shut it down. Kurtzman flew up to use the CIA's Cray III to try to make some sense out of the clues. You guys come up with anything on your way here?"

"No." Lyons answered for the group.

"The President has everyone working on this one. I've given the CIA, the FBI and the National Security Council a copy of this information. They have some of the best minds in the country working on solving the rhyme."

Ironman's jaw flexed as he gritted his teeth. "Was that really necessary?"

"Yes." Brognola said flatly. His eyes bore into Lyons's. "This isn't a personal vendetta, Carl. The stakes are too high. We're talking about the lives of several million people. The President has the entire military on alert, and his staff's been working around the clock."

"Man," Grimaldi said as he entered the room, "you have got to see those Black Hawks. Talk about state-of-the-art. Give me those babies for a few weeks and we could liberate Cuba."

"That's the upside," Brognola said. "For once the bean counters in Washington can't nickle and dime us. Right now we can get anything we need. You name it and it's yours, Carl."

"What have you got in a twenty-five-year-old blonde?" Pol asked as he leaned back in his chair. "Low mileage and," Blancanales cupped his hands behind his head, "lots a horsepower."

Nan punched Pol in the shoulder with all her might. The blow had enough impact to cause Pol to lose his balance. Both he and his chair toppled over backward. Pol, caught off guard, hit the floor with a thud. *"¿Qué pasa?"*

"Shit, I wish I'd done that," Brognola said with a grin.

For the first time since the model plane had buzzed the complex, a flicker of a smile broke across Ironman's face.

Pol jumped to his feet and tried to regain a measure of his dignity. "Hey, Gadgets, has your girlfriend had her shots?"

"You're on your own, Homes," Schwarz answered. "But I think you'd either better watch your mouth or learn how to keep your left up."

"Sorry," Nan said. "Reflex reaction."

"All right, all right," Brognola said as he motioned Pol back toward his chair. "Recess is over. We've got more pressing problems. We've got to find the answer to this puzzle."

EVERYONE IN THE COMPUTER ROOM ignored Aaron Kurtzman, which was just fine with him. The head of computer security for the CIA, a whining little bureaucrat named Winslow, had tried to deny Bear access to the Company's mainframes and data bases. A phone call from the White House had shown him the advantages of interagency cooperation.

The main room was stark. Thirty identical desks, in six rows of five each, faced the glass-enclosed computer room. Thirty identical computer terminals were on the same corner of each desk. Thirty men and women were busy at their keyboards. Bear had been given the use of one of the two private offices at the rear of the room.

Kurtzman glanced out the window at the people laboring away and shook his head. The CIA, since Watergate, had relied more and more on electronic information gathering and less on men in the field. Spy satellites, listening devices and an army of people poring over foreign newspapers had replaced field operatives. The technocrats who had taken over could generate a mountain of facts and figures. In 1979 they knew the exact weight of the Iranian caviar harvest, but no one knew that the Shah was in trouble.

Covert had become a nasty word at Langley. And for good reason. With former agents writing best-sellers and others trading secrets to cover their condo payments and bar tabs, the operative was an endangered species. The career staff knew that they would never be embarrassed by a spy satellite's testimony before a Senate subcommittee. The fewer people and the more machines the better.

"Pretty gruesome, huh?" Barbara McLane said. Unlike her boss, Winslow, McLane relished Bear's company. Perched on the end of her desk, she had followed Kurtzman's eyes out into the processing center. "Everyone out there has at least a Ph.D."

"You're kidding," Bear said as he surveyed the room again.

"Some of the best minds in the country," Barbara McLane added with a laugh. "Half of them couldn't find their way to the bathroom without a map."

"No common sense?"

"No," McLane said, pouring herself another cup of coffee. She held up the pot, and Bear pushed his cup toward the edge of the desk. "College groupies. Most of these people hung out on campus till they ran out of courses to take. Then we hired them here. These jokers have never had a real job or spent fifteen minutes in the real world. Anyone with talent and brains burns out after about three years in this zoo. You see what's left—the lifers. Some the best-trained paper shufflers money can buy."

"I understand." Bear blew on the top of his cup before taking a sip. "This, by the way, is the worst coffee I've ever tasted."

"Thanks. It's an old family recipe." McLane was a plump brunette in her early forties. "About two-thirds of the people out there are career bureaucrats. I honestly think they believe they get their pension based on how much paper they use."

"Why do you keep them?"

"That's a laugh," McLane said as she sampled her coffee. She curled her nose and reached for the non-dairy creamer. "We can't fire any of them, so we try to move them to nonvital areas till they get their twenty years in."

"What happens then?"

"They move on to the public sector and qualify for another pension plan. Most of these people are double dippers, and there are even a few triple dippers."

"Double dippers and triple dippers? Sounds like ice cream."

"Just as sweet. They'll take a civil service scoop, a military retirement scoop, and some even collect Social Security."

"That would be the triple dipper?"

"Right." McLane tried her coffee again, then reached for a packet of sugar. "You're right about the coffee. I can't understand it. It was fine yesterday."

Kurtzman had taken an immediate liking to Barbara McLane. Instead of being upset that an outsider had usurped her desk, she was grateful for the company. Instead of throwing up the normal roadblocks and stalls, which he had expected, she had been very helpful.

"Hey, I have an idea." McLane reached for the keyboard. "We're not getting anywhere with the riddle. Let's take a different approach."

"I'm all ears."

"Well, from what you've told me about Queensbury, he's probably had someone watching your team every step of the way. Right?"

"Okay," Bear said without following where she was headed. "But my guys would have picked up the tail."

"I agree," McLane said with a smile. "But you don't have to tail anyone if you know where they're headed."

"Oh, so you think he may have had someone watching the lab and the house, and someone else watching the campus?"

"Right."

"Interesting, but I don't see how that information could help him."

McLane's eyes twinkled. "What if they called Queensbury with a progress report?"

A light flashed on for Kurtzman. "Then there would be a long-distance call from each location to the same number."

"Exactly. Fortunately both areas are rather small. There couldn't have been that much long-distance activity."

"It's worth a shot."

"Right now it's the only game in town."

BROGNOLA HAD SCRAWLED the riddle from the Gamesmaster on the blackboard. Everyone sat in silence, staring at the words. For the first hour they traded many ideas, none of them the solution to the riddle. During the second hour the conversation began to lag. Now, after three hours in the war room, they were no closer to solving the riddle than when they'd first sat down.

"How about ...?" Gadgets said, breaking the silence. "Naw." The library calm returned.

Stained coffee cups and crumpled wads of paper formed burial mounds in various corners of the room. Nan Stein rolled her fingertips on the top of the conference table until she noticed that everyone was staring. Her face darkened slightly and her hands dropped to her lap. After a few moments of silence, she began to hum a John Denver tune.

Gadgets jumped up as if he had sat on a tack. "That's it!" He kissed Nan full on the lips and did a short war dance.

"What?" the stunned woman demanded.

"That song you were humming!" Gadgets looked around the room. All he saw were blank stares.

"I think Gadgets has gone bye-bye," Pol said.

Brognola refused to get his hopes up after so many blind alleys. "What have you got, Gadgets?"

"Don't you see? It's the song Nan was humming. John Denver." Gadgets began to hum the tune and encouraged the others to join in.

"I wouldn't give up my day job, old buddy," Pol said.

"You guys are missing the point. It's the lyrics of the song."

"You're right!" Nan said as she jumped to her feet and hugged Gadgets. Ignoring his painful ribs, Gadgets grabbed Nan around the waist and spun her off her feet. "It was so simple," she said, kissing the electronics whiz on the cheek.

"Too easy. That's why we missed it."

"What?" the others demanded.

"If," Gadgets said, beaming, "you asked John Denver where 'almost heaven' was, what would he answer?"

Pol slapped his forehead. "West Virginia!"

17

"There." Barbara McLane pointed to a number on the screen.

"It's a 304 area code."

McLane pulled a phone book out of her desk drawer and turned to the page with long-distance dialing codes. "West Virginia."

"Can we narrow it down?"

"Sure," McLane's fingers danced across the keyboard. "It's a rural exchange near the small town of Lockwood."

"Have you got a map?"

McLane picked up her phone and pushed four buttons for an inside line. "Wilson? This is McLane downstairs. I need a map of West Virginia, and I mean *now*. Bring me everything you've got."

She hung up and chuckled. "I love it. Wilson is one of those lifers I've told you about. He's only six months away from retirement. I understand he won't even take a crap here because he's afraid it might offend someone. I imagine you don't have many like him in your organization."

Bear shrugged. He wasn't going to discuss anything about the Farm with anyone from the CIA. McLane seemed decent enough, but there was always a chance she had an ulterior motive behind her helpfulness. Unless he knew exactly who he was talking to, Kurtzman wouldn't even admit that Stony Man existed.

"The number belongs to a—I don't believe this," McLane said. "It belongs to a Queensmaster Motion Picture Company. This guy really has balls."

"Yes, but he may have made his first mistake. I'll need a secured line."

McLane pointed to three red phones on the credenza behind her desk. "Take your pick."

Before Kurtzman could move, a pudgy little man with a nervous twitch tapped on the closed office door. Under his arm were several large rolled-up maps. McLane motioned him in.

"Here are the maps you wanted, Ms. McLane. Will there be anything else?"

"No, that will be fine." McLane cleared a space on her desk and unrolled one of the maps. "Here it is— Lockwood."

"Hello." Bear ran his finger down the map. "What have we here? The New River and the Meadow River. And, surprise surprise, the Meadow ends about two miles from Lockwood. I have to get hold of Brognola." Before he could reach for one of the secured telephones, the one in the middle began to ring. "Should I answer it?"

"Sure. It's probably for you."

She was right. Hal Brognola was on the line.

"We've broken the first part of the code."

"I know. West Virginia."

"What? How?" the head Fed asked incredulously.

"We backtracked through the phone company's long-distance records. We also have a phone number and an address."

ALFRED POTTS LICKED his lips as he watched the information change on his screen. He swiveled slowly in his chair, keeping his eyes on the monitor for as long as possible.

"Someone's been checking our phone number, Gamesmaster."

Queensbury was busy applying heavy pancake makeup. "About time. I suppose it wasn't fair to plant that virus in Able Team's computer system. This time loss has really hurt their chances of beating the time limit."

"Well," Potts said, "this contest is between you and Carl Lyons. You just stopped someone from helping him."

Queensbury nodded. "Good point, Alfred. Call the men in. Our guests should be arriving within two hours."

"Yes, sir." Potts scurried away into the darkness of the cave.

The four men from the raid on BioTech—Sonny and B. J. Hayes, Bubba Jones and Woody Woods— wandered into the control area. Sonny Hayes pulled up the only available chair, sat down and began cleaning his fingernails with the point of a pocket-knife. The rest of the men leaned on the computer console.

"You understand the game?" Queensbury asked.

The four men nodded.

"Sonny, are you sure about the two men at the shed?"

Hayes refused to make eye contact with Queensbury. Sonny had taken an instant disliking to the pudgy genius. Queensbury had sprung him from prison and he paid well, but that was where it ended. No friendship. No loyalty.

"I've known those boys for a long time. They'll do."

"Excellent," the Gamesmaster said. "In a few minutes I'll set off the charge that will seal the main entrance to the tunnel. At that point there will only be two ways in or out. I've already deposited a hundred thousand dollars in each of your Swiss accounts. The one who kills Carl Lyons will receive a million-dollar bonus."

"APPARENTLY," Brognola said to Lyons, "the New River is one of the oldest rivers in the United States."

"Which would explain the part of the riddle, 'Where New is old.'"

"And the Meadow River is only a few miles away."

"Which would explain why New and Meadow were capitalized." Brognola turned at the sound of an approaching helicopter. "That should be Bear with the maps."

Lyons checked his watch. It was 8:00 a.m. He only had six hours left, and one of those was needed to travel from Stony Man to Lockwood. "Can we be briefed in transit?"

"I don't know. Let's ask Kurtzman."

Several men were lifting Aaron Kurtzman, electric wheelchair and all, out of the helicopter. In his lap were several maps and an off-white box about the size of two shoe boxes. The wind had a nasty nip and an occasional snowflake drifted down. The ground was still too warm for any of the white stuff to stick, but in a few hours it would be a different story.

"Can the men be briefed in the air?" Brognola asked the computer genius.

"Sure," Bear answered. "We'll have to take one of the Black Hawks."

"Thank you," Grimaldi said as he joined the group. "I've been dying to fly one of those babies."

Brognola shoved a fresh cigar into his mouth. "Those helicopters came equipped with pilots, Grimaldi," the big Fed said, turning to his ace pilot.

"Put them in the other one," Lyons suggested in a voice barely audible above the sound of the beating rotor of the helicopter that had brought Bear home. "I want Jack to fly our bird."

"It's your call this time, Carl," Brognola answered.

"All right. Thanks, Ironman." Grimaldi gave a thumbs-up and headed toward the hangar. In a matter of moments two General Electric T700 turbo-shaft engines whined to life. The four blades of the rotor started slowly, but quickly picked up speed.

"Like a kid with a new toy," Brognola muttered. "Speaking of toys, what's that thing in your lap, Bear?"

"It's a portable computer." Kurtzman patted the high-impact plastic case of his NEC PowerMate 40. "This baby isn't as sophisticated as my equipment, but with forty megabytes of hard disk and a modem I thought it might come in handy."

"This is the same piece of equipment you've asked for at least a dozen times, Kurtzman." Brognola said, spitting out a cigar fragment.

"Yeah, I know. Some young hotshot from the White House caught me as I was leaving Langley. You know the type—Ivy League, expensive suit, red silk tie. He asked me if there was anything I needed. I had it before I reached the helipad."

"Did you sign anything?"

"Nope. I think he took it off some poor guy's desk. Look." Bear held up the portable computer. Mounted on the bottom was a thin metal plate with an embossed inventory control number.

Brognola shook his head. "I don't think we'll have any trouble removing that. Good work."

"Yeah, and here's the real kicker. The previous owner didn't have time to erase the memory in the hard drive. No telling what we might find."

Pol and Gadgets, carrying oversize nylon bags, came out of the armory. Schwarz's face was red. Carrying the heavy bags made his injured ribs throb, but he wasn't about to admit it. Nan Stein, empty-handed and wide-eyed, followed behind.

"I've never seen so many weapons and explosives in my life," the attractive toxicologist said. "You guys expecting the Russian army?"

"Should have seen it before the last garage sale," Pol answered.

"Careful," Gadgets warned. "Remember what happened the last time you opened your smart mouth. Nan here closed it for you."

"Sorry there, little lady," Pol said while attempting a John Wayne impersonation. "I didn't mean no offense."

"Is he always like this?" she asked.

"No," Gadgets answered. "You were lucky and caught him on a good day."

"You must be Dr. Stein," Kurtzman said, extending his hand.

Nan took Bear's hand and gave it a firm squeeze. "We met briefly about a year ago."

"At the convention in New York."

"I'm flattered that you remembered."

"Well, actually," Bear said sheepishly, "it was in your file."

"Did you find her bra size yet?" Gadgets asked. Stein's face flushed and her nostrils flared. Gadgets leaned away from a right cross. The sudden move made his chest feel as if someone had stuck a knife between his ribs.

"You okay?" Nan asked, her anger replaced with concern.

"I'm fine."

"You think we should get you X-rayed, old buddy?" Pol asked.

"We don't have time. Besides, we've all played hurt before."

Pol nodded. The body could do amazing things when pumped up with enough adrenaline. Gadgets had earned the benefit of the doubt on his battle readiness.

"Let's load up," Ironman said. "Bear will brief us in the air as we head to West Virginia."

18

Sonny Hayes slammed a clip into his AK-47 and flipped the switch to full automatic. B. J. Hayes, Sonny's twin brother, was strapping additional clips to his thigh for the assortment of weapons he was carrying. While obviously brothers, they weren't identical twins. Sonny was slightly taller and B.J. was around twenty pounds heavier. Both had short-cropped blond hair, fair skin and pale blue eyes. Their first brush with the law had been when they were only thirteen. They had stolen, then wrecked a car. When Queensbury had found them by scanning through computerized prison records, they were doing life for a six-month crime spree through Arkansas that had left three people, including their partner, dead.

The brothers, along with Bubba Jones and Woody Woods, were exactly the type of muscle Herbert Queensbury needed. They were all young, strong, fearless and functionally illiterate. Queensbury, with his superior intellect, was able to keep the men on a short leash. He knew each man's strengths and weaknesses. With the careful distribution of cash, women and drugs, Queensbury had kept the men under his thumb. Except for Sonny.

Sonny Hayes chafed under the whip of Queensbury.

"How much longer do you think it'll be, Sonny?" B.J. asked as he nervously fiddled with the Colt .45 his brother had just handed him.

"It won't be too long now, B.J."

"What you gonna do with the money, Sonny?"

"I'm gonna get me a house with a fishin' lake down by Hot Springs. Then I'm gonna get me a bass boat, a couple of new cars and a big-wheel pickup."

A puzzled look covered B.J.'s face. "You gonna get all that with a hundred thousand dollars?"

"No, baby brother." The corners of Sonny's mouth lifted into a menacing, wicked smile. "I'm plannin' on collecting the million."

FRANK JUDSON, the contractor who had done most of the work inside the coal mine, was the first to spot the helicopters. The snow was falling at a steady rate, and visibility had been cut to less than a quarter mile. The group waiting for Able team had heard the twin Black Hawks long before they had seen them.

Sheriff Jimmy Scales had left his emergency lights flashing to give the pilots of the helicopters an idea of where to land. The Black Hawks touched down on the loading area of the defunct Lucky Lady coal mine.

Scales, a lifetime resident of Lockwood and nearly sixty years old, walked with a pronounced limp. With the ruddy complexion of an outdoorsman and the general size and build of a professional wrestler, he had once been a formidable specimen. Time and booze had taken their toll. Leaning against the side of his car, he moved the wad of tobacco to the other side of his mouth and spit a black stream of juice onto the ground.

Scales was in the "screw you" stage of his career. After thirty-six years as sheriff, he could take full retirement anytime he wanted. He wasn't going to take a large ration of crap from anyone, including the governor. The phone call from the State House in Charleston had pissed him off but good. This was his county. The idea that the state and federal boys were coming in to show him how it should be done stuck in his craw.

Brognola sensed the tension instantly. Lyons was too intent on the mission to notice.

"I'm Brognola from Washington."

Scales neither extended his hand nor spoke. Instead, he fired another round of tobacco juice into the snow.

"Do you have the maps we requested?"

"Yeah," Scales muttered, pointing his thumb at the back of his police car. "Help yourself."

Lyons opened the rear door of the car and pulled out the maps. After unrolling the first one, his shoulders sagged. "These tunnels go for miles in all directions."

"This mine operated for over forty years," Scales said. "And that map's only the upper level. There are two more levels below that one."

"How many entrances are there?"

"Couple of dozen, but you make one wrong turn and you could wander around in there for days." Scales bounced a glob of tobacco juice off the police cruiser's front tire and wiped his chin with the back of his gloveless hand. "Somebody blasted the main entrance shut about an hour ago."

"Damn." Lyons slammed his fist down on the hood of the police car.

"I think I know how to get inside." The group turned toward the man carrying a set of blueprints under his arm.

"Who are you?" Brognola asked.

"Frank Judson. I'm the contractor who did the recent work inside the tunnel."

Moving to the helicopter and out of the snow, Judson spread out the blueprints of the work he had done in the coal mine. "We sealed up these tunnels, here, here and here."

"What did you use to seal them?" Gadgets asked.

"Two-by-fours and plywood mostly. Nothing permanent."

"How hard would they be to get through?"

"Like going through the exterior wall of a house. It could be done, but not without making a lot of noise."

"We can't go in that way," Lyons said.

"Why not?" Nan asked.

"Our job isn't to get into the mine. It's to find the toxin. If we start knocking down Queensbury's props, he'll get pissed off and might just take the toxin and leave."

Nan leaned forward and rested her elbows on her knees. "How would he get out?"

Judson laughed. "Ma'am, there's a hundred different ways out of that mine. The Gauley River has cut a gorge over a thousand feet deep on the back side of this hill. In the old days the miners would follow a seam of coal till they hit daylight. If you're willin' to get dirty, for every entrance that's on this map, I can show you ten that aren't."

"Is there a back way in?" Ironman asked.

"No," Judson answered. "This guy really did his homework. He had our crew block off every stray tunnel."

"How did you get involved with Queensbury?" Pol asked.

Judson shrugged. "Jobs have been hard to come by around here since the mine closed. They said they were from Hollywood and wanted to make a movie. They even had some PR guy come down from Charleston with a permit from the State Bureau of Mines. Seemed like an easy way to make a few bucks." Judson reached into his front shirt pocket and brought out the check Queensbury had given him.

"What's that?" Pol asked.

"A check from Mr. Parker. I don't reckon its worth the paper it's written on. It's gonna be a bleak Christmas around here."

"May I see that?" Brognola asked.

"Sure."

"We'd better take this as evidence, Mr. Judson. It may take a while, but I'll see if we can get you reimbursed."

Judson's face brightened. "That would be great, sir."

"What else," Lyons asked, getting the questions back on track, "did you do besides seal up the tunnels?"

"I ran a couple of miles of coaxial cable, ran some lights, installed video cameras, put up some speakers and built a big room."

Judson now had Ironman's interest. "Where's the room?"

Judson pointed to a spot on the upper level. "Right here."

Lyons studied the map for a moment. "What's the best way to get there?"

"Normally I'd say just go in the main entrance. Now I'd say go in here." Judson circled a spot on the map with a highlighter pen. "In fact, that may be the only way to get in without tearing down one of my walls.''

''What's this?''

''It's a tunnel that was opened on the lowest level down by the train tracks so that the coal didn't have to be hauled up one of the elevator shafts.''

''Let me guess,'' Lyons said. ''It's right across from the mouth of the Meadow River.''

''Yeah, as a matter of fact, it is. How'd you know that?''

''Across from the Meadow, you'll find your goal.''

HERBERT QUEENSBURY admired himself in the mirror. The wizard's hat was a nice touch. With the matching robe he felt like Merlin.

''Are you sure I should go, Gamesmaster?'' Alfred Potts asked.

''Of course,'' Queensbury answered, adjusting his hat again. ''I can work the master controls.''

Potts pulled a palm-sized communicator from his pocket and turned it on. ''Are you sure this will be able to pick up your signal?''

''Of course.''

Potts wasn't so confident. He knew the hills contained enough iron ore to block even commercial radio broadcasts. ''If you say so. Are we really going to dump this stuff into the storm?''

''For a game to be any fun, Alfred, there must be a winner and a loser.'' Queensbury placed his arm around Potts's shoulders. ''Besides, after the sleeping gas wears off, imagine the uproar. You may sin-gle-handedly stop the manufacture of chemical weapons not only in the U.S. but around the world.''

''Then I'll be famous?''

''Your name will go down in history.'' Queens-bury neglected to mention that Potts would be on the same page with Hitler, Stalin and Mao. Potts na-ively thought the substance in the canisters was a harmless sleeping gas whose effect would wear off in a few hours. Instead, the moment he released the toxin he would move to the top of the list of the greatest mass murderers of the twentieth century.

''Run along now. If you don't hear from me in—'' Queensbury checked his watch ''—two hours and fourteen minutes, take off.''

Potts nodded. He flopped into the driver's seat of one of the two golf carts he and Queensbury used to move around in the tunnels and disappeared into the gloom.

Queensbury took his position at the console. In front of him was a bank of surveillance monitors. From his chair, with the flip of a switch, he could see nearly the entire length of the gauntlet Carl Lyons would have to run to capture him. On the center screen Queensbury saw the Hayes brothers moving into an ambush position near the elevator shaft.

''Excellent,'' Queensbury muttered. ''I wonder where the other two are?'' Queensbury flipped through the screens, trying to locate Jones and

Woods. He found them a few hundred yards from the lower-level entrance. "Idiots."

Queensbury pushed a switch on the console. "Back away from the entrance." Queensbury's voice reverberated throughout the tunnels. On the screen he saw Bubba and Woody jump at the unexpected sound of his voice.

"What the...?" Jones cried, fumbling for his weapon.

"I gave specific instructions," Queensbury said into the microphone on the console. "They are not to be killed until they're well into the tunnel."

Woods pointed in the direction of the concealed video camera and nudged Jones in the ribs. "He can see us."

"Sorry," Bubba said in too loud of a voice. "We'll back up."

POL PULLED Ironman aside. "You want me to tell him?"

Lyons shook his head. "No, I'll do it. Yo, Gadgets."

Schwarz jumped out of the helicopter and joined the rest of Able Team. "Yeah, what's up?"

"You're not going into the tunnel with us."

"What?"

"We may have to do some climbing, and with your ribs—"

"Look," Gadgets protested, "I've been hurt worse than this and still functioned well enough to pull your butt out of the fire.'' Gadgets had never questioned any of Ironman's battlefield decisions before. Then again, Lyons had never benched him before, either.

"Sorry, Homes," Pol said, "but I have to agree."

Schwarz's face flushed with anger. "What a load of BS."

"What's the problem?" Nan asked as she joined the group.

"They think a few cracked ribs is enough to put me out of action."

"Heck, hon." Nan put an arm around his waist. "Look at it this way. It's the first time these guys have left us alone."

Gadgets wiggled free of the scientist's arm. "I don't like it."

"Oh, grow up," Nan said, her eyes sparking. "These guys are your best friends. You think they don't want you to come along? You think they don't need you? You should be thanking them for making the decision you should have already made." She shoved her hands into her pockets and walked back toward the helicopter. Under her breath she muttered, "Macho jerk."

Gadgets knew she was right. In the twelve hours since his Kevlar vest had stopped the .380 slug, his body had started the healing process. His muscles had tightened and the work by his internal repair crew had sapped his strength. He could barely lift his hands above his head, and every time he inhaled he saw stars.

"Okay. I stay here. I don't like it, but I stay. So what's the plan?"

Lyons reached for a long rope and threw it over his shoulder. "It's time to pay Herbert Queensbury a visit."

QUEENSBURY, still sitting at the control console, rotated the oscillator that dimmed the lights throughout the tunnels. Not only did he like the subdued effect, it would give his men a slight edge. They would be able to blend into the shadows. He checked his watch. It was time. Queensbury licked his lips in anticipation as he activated the custom-designed ruby lasers. He couldn't wait to see the look on Lyons's face.

Queensbury stepped up onto the stage. The area was bathed in light, and it took a moment for his eyes to adjust to the brightness. He located the spot on the floor that Potts had marked for him with masking tape. Reaching above his head, he adjusted the microphone that was attached to a long boom arm.

Queensbury was ready to give the greatest performance of his life. He was ready to bring the house down.

19

For over a million years, with the spring thaw, the Gauley, the New and the Meadow rivers had roared through the mountains of central West Virginia. They had carved narrow valleys, some over a thousand feet deep, through sheer rock. The land wasn't suitable for farming and most of the good timber had been removed a century earlier and the area never reforested. If not for the abundance of coal, the mountain area of the state would still be wilderness. A century earlier, to fuel a growing nation, men had come to West Virginia to spend twelve hours a day underground in poorly ventilated mines. To move the coal railroads had been constructed. The only logical path for the iron horse was to follow the banks of the rivers.

Jack Grimaldi had the Black Hawk in the air, looking for a place to land. His choices were limited. He found a level spot near the lower entrance to the Lucky Lady mine where rail cars had once been loaded. The rotors on the big Sikorsky were sixty-five feet from tip to tip. The spot Grimaldi had selected wasn't much larger.

"You're not going to try to land there, are you?" Captain Peter Metzger asked. Metzger wasn't happy about giving up the controls of his helicopter, but his orders had been clear. Whatever these guys wanted they got. He had at least convinced Grimaldi to let him ride in the front gunner seat. Still, he had no intention of letting the Able Team pilot wreck the Black Hawk without getting his two cents in.

"It'll be a tight squeeze, but we'll fit."

"Right." Metzger cinched his seat belt tighter and braced his hands on the control dash.

The big Sikorsky touched down as gently as a feather with room to spare. About six inches of room.

"I wouldn't have believed it if I hadn't seen it myself," Metzger said.

"Piece of cake," Grimaldi said as he shut down the rotor.

Lyons already had the side door open and was on the ground. Pol began handing him the equipment they would need and Ironman began stacking it neatly on the ground. Each man would be carrying about thirty pounds of gear in addition to their weapons.

Gadgets was the odd man out. There were only two backpacks instead of three; Pol and Ironman would be going into the tunnel without him. It was a new experience for Gadgets, and it left him feeling old and useless.

"Penny for your thoughts."

Gadgets turned to see Nan's smiling face. "You wouldn't get your money's worth."

"You want to go, don't you?"

Gadgets laughed. "Is it that obvious?"

"'Fraid so. You'd just be a liability in the tunnel."

Gadgets sighed. "I know. I just wish there was something I could do."

"Welcome to the club. Pol's okay, but him—" Nan hooked her thumb over her shoulder in the direction of Lyons "—what a jerk."

"Intense. This is personal for him."

"Then he's not always like this?"

"Well," Gadgets said, scratching his head, "let's just say he's not always quite as intense."

If Ironman's ears were burning, he didn't show it. He methodically packed the mountain climbing gear into his backpack and slung a length of heavy rope over his shoulder.

"Do you think we'll need all of this?" Pol asked as he adjusted the straps on his backpack.

"I hope not." Lyons checked his watch. "We've got an hour and twenty-one minutes to get to the room."

"Ironman," Pol said softly, "what if the toxin isn't in the room?"

"Then a whole lot of people are going to die."

CLIMBING TO THE ENTRANCE of the tunnel was tricky. The seam of coal the miners had followed hit daylight about a hundred feet above the Gauley River. Time and weather had long since rotted away the chute that had delivered the coal to the train cars. The swirling snow coated the rocks and a stiff wind cut visibility.

Blancanales lost his grip and slid ten feet down the face of a smooth rock.

"You okay?" Ironman asked, tossing Pol a rope.

"The only thing hurt is my pride, Ironman." Pol grabbed the rope and pulled himself up to the ledge where his partner was waiting. "This is harder than it looks."

"We're almost there." Ironman recoiled the rope and continued his ascent.

The timbers that had sealed the lower entrance of the Lucky Lady mine had recently been moved.

"Looks like he knew we were coming," Pol said, .pulling on the night vision glasses that hadn't been destroyed during the power station raid.

"Let's not keep him waiting." Lyons pushed several buttons on his Japanese-made sports watch.

"What are you doing, Ironman?" Pol asked.

"This watch has a countdown stopwatch. When the beeper goes off, our time's up." Ironman pushed the button on his wrist communicator. "Gadgets?"

"Yo."

"We're about to go in."

"What do you want me to do?"

"Stay in radio contact and be loose. No telling what'll happen next."

"Don't forget the relay unit."

"Pol's taking care of it right now."

Blancanales placed a black box, slightly larger than a shoe box, on the ground near the mouth of the tunnel. He flipped a switch and extended the antenna. "The unit's active."

"Great." Gadgets's voice came through the wrist communicator with added force. "That should add enough to your signal so that we won't lose contact."

"This is a big place," Ironman said, not convinced.

"You'll probably fade in and out, but the booster should help. Break a leg, guys. And remind Pol not to jump on any more grenades, okay?"

"Hadn't planned on it, Homes," Pol said into his communicator.

Lyons and Blancanales disappeared into the gloom of the abandoned coal mine. There was no time for finesse. The two Able Team warriors charged ahead, weaving from side to side and staying low. They knew they were targets, but that didn't mean they had to be sitting ducks. A hundred yards ahead there was a faint light.

"What do you make of that?" Lyons asked.

"I don't see anything, Ironman." Blancanales scanned the area ahead with the special eyes he had borrowed from Gadgets. "That doesn't mean it's not a trap. It's also the only way in."

"Nut up and do it."

As the two men swiftly closed the distance, the light grew brighter.

"Son of a bitch!" Lyons roared as he flipped off the safety on his M-16/203 combo.

"What?" Pol said, arriving next to Ironman.

"It's Queensbury."

"Where?"

"Right in front of you," Lyons barked.

Blancanales adjusted the night vision glasses and peered ahead. "All I see is a column of light."

"Take off those damn glasses."

As soon as the night vision glasses were removed, the column of light vanished and Herbert Queensbury stood a few yards ahead. "I don't like this, Ironman. Look through these." Pol handed the glasses to Lyons.

Ironman held them to his eyes without bothering to pull the contraption over his head. "What do you make of this, Pol?"

"Probably some kind of light projection. I've heard you can make a holograph with a laser. The glasses filter out whatever optical trick Queensbury's trying to pull. We could ask Gadgets—"

"No time. Let's go."

Lyons and Blancanales advanced on opposite sides of the tunnel. The passage widened into a large cavern that had once been a wide seam of coal. The projection of Herbert Queensbury was in the middle of the room.

"Welcome!" Queensbury said. His voice came from nowhere and everywhere. "You and your friend are most welcome. No need for introductions, Carl. This must be Rosario Blancanales. I see that Gadgets isn't here. Are his ribs still bothering him?"

"This place is wired like crazy," Pol whispered to Lyons. "Video cameras, microphones, and the system he's using to make this projection."

"You can pinpoint everything with those glasses?"

"Yeah, the equipment's giving off enough heat so that it sticks out like a sore thumb."

"At the first sign of danger, take all of it out."

"Roger."

"All right, Queensbury, I know you can see me," Lyons said as he stepped into the middle of the room. "State your business."

"My, my, we haven't changed a bit. Of course, you're aware of the time."

"Cut the crap, Queensbury, and get to the bottom line. You wouldn't have gone to all of this trouble if you didn't have something you wanted to say."

"The laconic Carl Lyons." Queensbury removed his wizard's hat and flipped it aside. As soon as it was out of range of the cameras that were producing the three-dimensional image, the hat seemed to vanish into thin air. "You're correct. I do have something to say. Every day I was in prison I thought of you, Carl. At first I planned to kill you slowly. Then I realized that would do no good. You'd gladly face death and never give me the satisfaction of watching you beg. So I came up with a better idea. What would hurt you more than death? Failure. Your ego would punish you every day of your life if your failure caused the death of millions of people.''

"You'd kill millions of innocent people just to get even with me?''

"Of course.''

"You're sick, Queensbury.''

Queensbury's eyes narrowed and his nostrils flared. "And *you* are very nearly out of time.''

"If I can reach you before the time limit expires, will you return the toxin?''

"You, of all people, should know that I always play fair. If you can reach this room before the time expires, I'll return the toxin.''

"And go back to prison?''

"What?'' Queensbury took a step backward, causing the holographic image to distort.

"You're the one who always thinks in terms of winning and losing. If we play by your rules and I get the toxin back, this game ends in a tie. If I don't, I lose. Where's the risk for you?''

"Why, I, ah,'' the Gamesmaster stammered.

"Come on, Herbie,'' Lyons taunted. "Make a real game of it. If you lose, you go back to prison.''

"Look at the time, Carl. You haven't got a chance.''

"Make the wager or return the toxin."

Herbert Queensbury's face flushed. "You're the most annoying man in the world."

Lyons walked toward one of the video cameras. The camera's autofocus lens purred softly. "Do we have a wager or not?"

"Damn you!" Queensbury's words reverberated off the walls of the mine.

"Say it, Herbie, or I'll pack up my tent and go home. I won't play a one-sided game."

"I'll release the toxin."

"No, you won't." Ironman's cold blue eyes stared directly into the video camera. "That wouldn't satisfy you. You want me to go through hell trying to reach you. Either agree to the terms or I won't play."

"Damn you! I agree!"

20

The internal area of the mine was crisscrossed with low, narrow tunnels that had linked the seams of coal. Bubba Jones was hidden behind a foot-thick wooden support that prevented the roof of one of the connecting tunnels from collapsing. Woody Woods had used the barrel of his AK-47 to shatter the bulbs of the lights that Queensbury had installed. Darkness was a sniper's best friend.

Woods took up his position a few yards behind Jones. "They should be here anytime," he whispered to his partner.

"Shh, I think I heard something."

The two men fell silent. Both heard the sounds of approaching footsteps.

POL GRABBED Ironman's arm to slow his pace. "I don't like this." The area head was dark; all the other passages had been well-lit.

"Look." Ironman motioned toward the right with the barrel of his M-16. Both men examined the broken glass of a light bulb on the ground. "I smell a trap."

The connecting tunnel ahead was less than a hundred feet long and had been gouged out of solid stone. A rusty set of tracks, designed to carry coal, ran along the floor. With the supporting timbers and natural crevices, there were a dozen ideal sniper positions.

"You see anything with those glasses?"

Pol moved into a better position near the entrance of the tunnel and peered into the darkness. "I've got one, no, two, hiding in there," he whispered. "One's about halfway down on the right. The other's a few yards behind him on the left."

Lyons looked into the darkened area and saw nothing. "You sure?"

"Here, look for yourself."

Lyons held the night vision glasses to his eyes. The tunnel, which was dark to the naked eye, was now as bright as midafternoon. He located the two targets.

"What do you propose, Ironman?"

Lyons handed Pol back his fancy headgear. "Do you think a grenade would bring down the roof of the tunnel?"

"If it does, we're finished. We'd never have time to pick our way through."

"They don't know they've been spotted." Ironman flipped his M-16 to autoburn. "Pin them down."

Pol dashed ahead of Ironman and fell prone on the ground, using one of the railroad ties for cover. He flipped the switch on his M-16 so that it would fire in 3-round bursts. The first man, hearing Pol coming, poked his head out from behind the timber that was protecting him. Blancanales opened fire. Three slugs tore into the wood, sending splinters flying. The hidden killer ducked back just in time. The second man leaned around the rock that he was using for cover and received the same greeting from Pol.

Lyons used the opportunity to storm the tunnel. For the next five seconds he would be in no-man's-land. If Pol's weapon jammed, he was history. Every time either of the two enemies tried to get into position to fire, they were chased back to cover by Blancanales.

The man using the wooden support for cover heard Ironman approaching and fired blindly in the general direction of the Able Team warrior. The 7.62 mm full metal jackets ricocheted off the walls, ceiling and floor of the tunnel. One bullet, flattened to the size of a quarter after hitting the wall, grazed Lyons on the thigh but Ironman ignored the pain. When he was less than ten feet from the enemy's position, he dived headlong to the ground. As he slid past the timber that the big man had been using for protection, Ironman's weapon roared to life. Lyons cut a tight autoburn figure eight. Six 5.56 mm slugs ripped into the terrorist's chest. He was dead before he hit the ground.

"You bastard!" his friend shouted. Lyons was in a vulnerable position when the man stepped from the shadows; he was staring down the business end of an impatient AK-47. "I'm gonna blow your head clean—"

A 3-round burst from Pol cut the conversation short. The first bullet hit the goon just above the left eye, taking out the rear of his skull as it exited. The second round hit him in the throat and the third in the upper chest. The force of the impact slammed his body against the tunnel wall. His weapon clattered to the floor, and he crumpled forward into a bloody heap.

"Nice of him to be so chatty," Pol said, kicking the pair of AK-47s down the tunnel. He checked both men for a pulse; he wasn't surprised when he didn't find one. "Do you know these guys?"

Lyons shook his head. As he tried to get up, his right leg buckled.

"You hit?"

"I took a rebound off the wall."

Pol pulled a knife from his boot and cut the coarse material of Ironman's pants. "It didn't break the skin, but you've got a major league bruise. Not much I can do for you, Ironman."

Lyons gritted his teeth as he forced the leg to respond. As the jolt of firefight adrenaline began to wear off, the leg started to throb. "I'll be all right."

Pol's wrist communicator began to vibrate. It was a new feature Gadgets and Cowboy Kissinger had added; no telltale beep or blinking light to give away a position.

Pol pushed the button on the side of the communicator, "Yo."

"We heard gunfire," Gadgets said.

"Able Team two, bad guys nothing."

Before Gadgets had a chance to ask any more questions, the voice of Herbert Queensbury boomed through the tunnels. "Very well done, Carl."

"What the hell was that?" Gadgets's voice asked over the device.

"Queensbury's got this place wired for sound and video," Lyons said. "There are speakers, microphones and cameras everywhere."

"Hmm," Gadgets answered.

"You got an idea?"

"Maybe. I'll get back to you."

THE SNOW HAD REDUCED visibility to a few hundred feet. From the floor of the valley cut by the Gauley River, the surrounding hills appeared to climb endlessly into swirling white clouds.

"What have you got in mind?" Nan asked as she tried to stomp some feeling back into her feet.

"I'm not sure. Where's Jack?"

"He's with the Air Force guy in the helicopter."

"Come on," Gadgets said. "We're going for a ride."

"We are?"

Gadgets slid the side door of the Black Hawk open and helped Nan aboard. "I want to take a look around the area, Jack."

"In this weather you won't see much." Grimaldi flipped a few switches on the console and the helicopter's rotor began to whine. "What are we looking for?"

"I'm not sure."

"But you'll know it when you see it, right?"

"That's about it."

"Oh, well, it's better than sitting around here freezing our nuts off." When the rotors were up to speed, the Black Hawk lifted off the ground. Strong winds funneling through the valley buffeted the helicopter until it reached the rim of the gorge. "What now?"

"Is there some kind of standard search pattern?"

"Sure. Is the object large or small?"

"Large."

"It's large, but you don't know what it is?" Grimaldi shook his head. "Is it in a fixed position?"

"Yeah."

"Then I'd recommend a square search pattern," Grimaldi said. "But with the limited visibility we won't be able to cover much territory with each pass."

Captain Metzger turned around in his chair. "We have some top-of-the-line radar and infrared imaging on this bird. What are we looking for?"

Gadgets leaned into the cockpit. "New construction and, most likely, some heavy power lines."

Grimaldi smiled broadly. "Gadgets, you dog, are you going to do what I think you're going to do?"

Stein and Metzger exchanged puzzled looks. Gadgets winked at Grimaldi. "Just because I'm on the injured reserve list doesn't mean I can't get back into the game."

The swirling snow made it necessary to concentrate on the landscape below, and a tense kind of quiet fell over the chopper.

"There!" Gadgets finally shouted, breaking the silence. The high winds had blown the camouflage netting off a yellow satellite dish.

Below was an ancient outbuilding that had obviously been abandoned when the mining company pulled out. The structure looked like a dozen others, weather-beaten and near the edge of collapse, that were scattered along the rim of the Gauley River gorge. There was one difference, however: newly strung power lines ran from the building to the nearest pole.

"That has to be it," Gadgets said, pointing at the building.

"What?" Nan demanded. "It looks like a tumbledown warehouse to me."

"That's what it's supposed to look like." Gadgets reached for an M-16/203 combo. "With all of the computer games Queensbury's been playing and the equipment he's installed in the tunnel, he must be using a ton of electricity. If we can knock out his eyes and ears, it might give Ironman and Pol a better chance. Jack, get me onto the ground.''

"Where are you going?" Nan demanded.

"Into that building," Gadgets answered.

"Not without me." Nan pulled an M-16/203 combo from the rack. The three men watched her in silence. She knew she was being tested. Calmly Nan pulled a bandolier of extra clips and grenades for the M-203 over her shoulder. Next she checked the breech of the M-16 before ramming a 20-round clip home. Like a veteran infantryman, she adjusted the sight of the M-203, pushed the loading chamber forward and placed a spin-stabilized 40 mm grenade into the launcher. "I'm ready if you are."

"I make it a habit never to say no to a heavily armed woman. Give us air cover after we hit the ground."

Grimaldi gave Gadgets a thumbs-up and brought the Black Hawk in. There would be no element of surprise if anyone was in the warehouse. The twin turboshafts of the Sikorsky would see to that. Even over the building storm, the pounding pulse of the engines could be heard for miles.

Grimaldi selected a spot some two hundred yards from the building for the two to disembark. That distance, and the fact that they had ample cover, meant Gadgets and Nan wouldn't be sitting ducks. Stein and Schwarz were out of the door as soon as the big Sikorsky was within a few feet of the ground.

The Black Hawk peeled away and hovered at two hundred feet. Like a massive bird of prey, it was ready to strike at the first sign of movement.

Gadgets danced from rock to rock, with Nan staying one boulder behind. The building appeared deserted. The only footprints in the fresh snow were their own. If anyone was in the building, they hadn't been outside in the past three hours. The last boulder was twenty yards from the abandoned warehouse. Gadgets would have to make the final run in one open field dash.

"Cover me," he whispered as the breathless doctor joined him.

Using the rock as a bipod, she aimed her weapon at the long, low building. She would have to be on her toes because there were over a dozen windows that had good firing positions. Her hands were shaking and her mouth was dry as she watched Gadgets sprint across the open lot.

Gadgets heard the sound of breaking glass. Looking up, he saw the muzzle of an AK-47 protrude from a window. It was aimed directly at him.

The Able Team warrior tried to take evasive action by turning hard to the right. The snow had drifted over a rock about ten feet from the door. Schwarz's toe found the stone, and he lost his balance, landing hard on the ground. The AK-47 opened fire. The bullets sailed over his head as he tumbled.

His cracked ribs absorbed most of the impact. The unexpected fall and the sudden flash of pain momentarily stunned him.

Through the haze of pain, Schwarz's eyes focused on the barrel of the AK-47 that was still visible. It was aimed directly at him. Gunfire shattered the winter calm. He waited for the pain, but it didn't arrive.

"Are you hit?" Nan shouted.

The entire window where the sniper had been standing was now gone. The AK-47 lay harmless in the snow. Through the open window Gadgets could see the bullet-riddled body of his would-be assassin. Nan had saved his life.

Gadgets scrambled to his feet and pressed his back to the rough wood of the building. With a thumbs-up, he indicated to Nan that he was okay. Inside, he heard a desperate voice.

"Gamesmaster! Gamesmaster! Come in, come in!"

Gadgets popped his head up for a quick peek. The only living person in the room was a hard-looking black man standing by a desk with an intercom. In one hand was a microphone; in the other a Colt .45 automatic.

"Drop the weapon," Gadgets shouted, using the windowsill to steady his weapon. He had the M-16 set on autoburn and he wasn't about to take no for an answer.

The man dropped the microphone instead of the Colt. Before he could get the powerful handgun leveled, Gadgets opened fire. Round after round slammed into the big man's chest, but he refused to go down. After what seemed like minutes, he did a contorted death dance before landing on the desktop. As he died, he managed to fire one round in a final act of defiance. The bullet tore a gaping hole in the ancient wooden floor.

"This is the Gamesmaster," an annoyed voice said. "And this had better be important. I told you not to disturb me."

Gadgets stepped through the open window and picked up the microphone. "Sorry to be such a pest."

"Who is this?" the scratchy voice of Herbert Queensbury demanded.

"This is Hermann Schwarz. I'm a friend of Carl Lyons. I hope you brought a flashlight."

In the corner of the room Gadgets found the main power junction for Queensbury's underground complex. Instead of pulling the fuses, he pulled the trigger. Sparks leaped from the gray junction boxes as the bullets from Schwarz's M-16 severed the high-powered lines. One of the thick cables pulled free from its coupling and whipped around, sending out a spray of sparks. The dry boards of the old warehouse smoldered, then burst into flames. Gadgets made no attempt to extinguish the dozens of small fires that broke out. Instead, he climbed back through the shattered window, leaving the two bodies. Before he reached the Black Hawk, the building was engulfed in flames.

21

"What the hell?" B. J. Hayes roared as the lights in the tunnel flickered, then went out. With the loss of power a series of battery-operated emergency lights clicked on. Instead of the soft, even lighting, widely spaced, high-powered spotlights illuminated the tunnel. One of the spots was aimed directly at B.J. What had moments before been an ideal ambush position was now lit up like Times Square.

"Take cover, you idiot!" Sonny Hayes hissed at his brother. "They could be here anytime."

"Sorry, Sonny," B.J. answered, moving to a spot behind a rock and closer to the elevator. "Is this okay?"

Sonny lined his brother up in the sights of his AK-47 and feinted as if he was going to pull the trigger. "That's fine, little brother."

B.J. turned and saw the weapon pointed in his direction. "Don't kid around, Sonny."

Sonny Hayes lowered the AK-47 and burrowed deeper into a crevice near the elevator shaft. If only his brother would realize that he wasn't kidding. It was because of B.J.'s stupidity that they had ended up in jail. He had always been the brains and B.J. the brawn. Now he had the chance to make a cool million and nothing, not even his own brother, was going to stand in the way.

Sonny leaned out of his hiding place and let fly a stream of black tobacco juice from the wad he'd been chewing. He had positioned himself behind his brother and with a clear sight line to the approaching tunnel. B.J. didn't realize he was going to be caught in the cross fire. If B.J. got lucky and killed Lyons, he'd never collect the bonus from Queensbury. Sonny planned to shoot him in the back. Blood was thicker than water, but it wasn't thicker than a million bucks.

AT THE FIRST FLICKER of the lights Lyons and Blancanales leaped for cover in opposite directions. "Looks like Gadgets has been busy, Ironman."

Lyons glanced at his watch. "We've got less than twenty minutes."

"Yeah, I know. Hello." Pol and his night vision glasses were staring down the tunnel. "We've got company. I make one, now two snipers up ahead."

"We don't have time to play games with these guys."

"Grenades?"

"No," Lyons answered. "It might bring the roof down or damage the elevator. I have a better idea. Will those things work in total darkness?"

"Not very well. They'll pick up general shapes from the heat, but that's about it."

"Close enough."

Lyons braced his elbows on a large rock and drew a bead on one of the emergency lights. The crack of the M-16 was followed by the sound of breaking glass. The tunnel was noticeably darker. In rapid sequence Lyons knocked out as many of the lights as he could get an angle on. Ironman dropped the spent clip onto the tunnel floor and rammed a fresh one home.

"Take out the lights behind us, Pol. Let's put them in silhouette and not us."

"Right." Blancanales darted a few yards back down the tunnel and used the emergency lights for target practice. When he was finished, he rejoined Ironman. "You got a plan?"

"We don't have time for a plan," Lyons growled. "We've only got time to attack. Let's go."

Before Pol could react, Lyons was sprinting down the tunnel toward the snipers.

"Absolutely certifiable," Blancanales muttered to himself.

THE HAYES BROTHERS flinched as the crack of Ironman's M-16 reverberated around the tunnel. With each round fired, the tunnel grew increasingly darker.

"What are they doing?" B.J. whispered. His voice had the jagged edge of fear.

"Shut up!" Sonny hissed. "They must know we're here."

At the sound of the approaching footsteps B.J. panicked. Clicking his AK-47 to autoburn, he fired blindly in the general direction of the fast-approaching Lyons. None of the bullets found their target. They danced and skipped off the rock until they finally found a soft seam of coal to penetrate.

At the first sound of gunfire Lyons dived head-first to the floor of the tunnel and followed the trail of hot lead back to B.J.'s position. Firing on full-auto, Lyons cut a wicked figure eight in the general direction of the first sniper. B.J. was well protected behind a large rock, but one of Lyons's rounds ricocheted off the wall and caught B.J. in the fleshy part of his arm. The unexpected jolt of pain caused the sniper to drop his AK-47.

"Sonny," B.J. cried. "Sonny, I'm hit!"

Sonny Hayes was too busy to notice the pleading of his brother. In the dark he couldn't see Lyons, but from the muzzle-flashes of the firefight, he had a good idea of his opponent's location. Sonny opened fire. The noise in the tunnel was deafening as thirty rounds spit from the barrel of the AK-47.

Lyons, knowing his muzzle-flash had given away his position, had never stopped moving. Scrambling to his feet, he charged hard to the right side of the tunnel. In the darkness he rammed into a boulder with his knee and tumbled to the ground again. By the time Sonny Hayes had fired where he thought Ironman was, the big guy from Stony Man Farm had already moved ten feet. He was closing in fast on B.J.

Sonny Hayes slammed a fresh clip into his Soviet assault rifle and leaned out from the safety of the crevice. Before he could find Lyons, a 3-round burst from Pol's weapon raked across his chest. Blancanales had made it back to the firefight just in time. Using the hot barrel of the AK-47 as a guide, he had aimed for the middle of the blurry target. All three rounds had found their mark.

Sonny Hayes dropped his rifle and staggered forward, raising his hand to his chest. One of Pol's rounds had nicked the descending aorta. He pulled his hand away as he felt the warmth of his own blood pump from the gaping hole just under his heart.

"Sonny," B.J. sobbed, "you gotta help me."

But Sonny Hayes couldn't hear his brother. He wouldn't hear anything ever again.

Lyons followed B.J.'s sobs to the rock where the wounded man was hiding. The frightened sniper heard Ironman coming.

Losing his composure, B.J. stepped from his position of safety. "You shot me, you bastard," he cried, raising his gun to fire.

Lyons heard the rustling of B.J.'s clothing. He was caught in the open—too far from cover and too far away to reach B.J. before the man fired. Although he would have liked to have taken the killer alive, Lyons had no choice. He pulled the trigger on his M-16.

The body of B. J. Hayes danced and jerked as the bullets slammed into the middle of his chest. A gurgling sound escaped from his throat as he crumpled into a heap.

Pol, pulling a flashlight from his bag, provided the first light since the men had stepped into the dark killing zone.

"You okay, Ironman?"

"Yeah," he said with a sigh. "I just wish we could have taken one of them alive. No telling how many more are waiting for us."

"Queensbury only sprung four out of prison. Maybe we got them all."

"Maybe. Let's go. We don't have much time."

The two Able Team warriors sprinted toward the elevator that would take them to the upper level. Ironman pushed the up button, but nothing happened. "No power. We'll have to climb the cable."

"That's a four-hundred-foot climb."

"I know." Lyons checked his watch. "We'd better get started."

Using his flashlight, Pol located the trapdoor. Lyons cupped his hands and boosted Blancanales up through the opening. Pol scrambled up onto the roof of the disabled elevator.

"Holy..."

"What?" Lyons demanded.

"You've got to see this for yourself, Ironman."

Pol extended his arm through the trapdoor and grabbed Ironman's right wrist. With a grunt he pulled Lyons to the roof of the elevator.

"It's a good thing Gadgets blew out the power," Pol said.

"Why?"

Blancanales trained his light on a brick of plastique wired to the motor of the elevator. "I've got a feeling this elevator would have taken us higher than we expected. Like maybe up to the pearly gates."

Lyons nodded. There was no time to fathom why the fates had chosen this moment to smile on them. The clock was ticking. "Let's go."

Both men strapped a harness around their waists and pulled on a pair of belaying gloves. The harness hung loosely, but if they fell, the tension would be taken up by their thighs and buttocks. There would be no restrictions on the arms or upper body. The gloves were a split cowhide design that provided an excellent grip.

Lyons snapped his pair of ascenders on to the cable and slid his arms through the attached sling. He began to climb hand over hand. The ascenders, with built-in hand grips, made the climb easier. Not easy, just easier.

The Able Team warrior paused briefly to allow his tired arms a moment's rest. His face was covered with sweat and he was breathing hard through his mouth. "I see a light at the top of the shaft."

Pol, about twenty feet below Lyons, leaned to one side and looked up. "I see it, too. What do you think, another two hundred feet?"

Before Lyons could answer, the watch on his left wrist began to beep.

Time had run out.

22

The gasoline-powered generator purred softly as Herbert Queensbury plugged the cord from the public address system into one of the active outlets. His eyes gleamed as he blew on the microphone. "Testing, one, two, test." Satisfied, Queensbury made his fatal announcement.

"Carl, your time has run out. The game's over. You lose!"

Queensbury's words echoed throughout the tunnel complex. He knew that Lyons and Blancanales, dangling from the elevator cable, had heard the message loud and clear.

"No!" Lyons roared as he began to climb more quickly. The warriors of Able Team were close enough that Queensbury could hear Ironman's scream.

"Don't be a sore loser, Carl. You did much better than I expected." Queensbury pulled his wizard's cape over his head. Underneath he had on a very different costume—the uniform of a West Virginia state trooper. "Oh, you might want to head back down to the first level, Carl. I've placed a series of explosives on the support columns on this level. In about two minutes there won't be much left.''

''Wait!'' he heard Lyons scream at the top of his lungs. ''It's me you want. Why kill all those people?''

Queensbury adjusted his state trooper hat and smiled. ''Of course it's you I want, Carl. But if I killed you, your misery would be over.'' Queensbury moistened his lips. ''Instead, as you watch the body count rise, you'll know it was all your fault. What sweet revenge for my years in prison.''

Queensbury dropped the microphone and jumped behind the wheel of his golf cart. He knew exactly where he was headed—a hidden entrance dug by his own men. Wearing the highway patrol uniform he would be able to walk away unchallenged. He looked down at the center console of the golf cart and the radio remote activator that was located there. About the size of a pocket calculator, the unit would activate the charges planted throughout the mine. Queensbury extended the antenna and pushed the flashing red button. ''Goodbye, Carl,'' he said quietly.

''WHAT NOW, Ironman?'' Pol asked.

''Down and fast,'' Lyons ordered. ''We've got to get out of here and try to stop the toxin from being released.''

''Right.''

Both men untied themselves from the ascender slings and attached carabiners to the cables. Using the cable like a rappeling rope, both Pol and Iron-man went into a near free-fall. It took less than fif-teen seconds to drop the same distance it had taken ten minutes to climb. Standing on top of the eleva-tor, the two men unhooked themselves from the ca-ble.

"Weapons and flashlights only," Lyons said, re-moving his backpack and casting it aside. "We have to make time."

"Right." Pol jumped through the trapdoor, landed on all fours and rolled to break the fall. Ironman was half a beat behind.

"See if you can raise Gadgets and advise him of the situation." Overhead, they heard a distant rum-bling, and dust and pebbles began falling down the elevator shaft.

It took a few tries, but Blancanales finally heard the voice of his Able Team comrade.

"I can barely hear you, Pol," Gadgets shouted. "What was that explosion?"

"That's not important. Queensbury got away and we don't have the toxin. We'll be back at the en-trance in about fifteen minutes. Meet us there."

"WHAT ARE WE GOING to do?" Nan demanded.

"I honestly don't know," Gadgets answered softly.

"Well, we can't sit around here doing nothing."

"I'm open to suggestions."

"Let's go look for the toxin."

"Where?"

She didn't have an answer. Nan folded her arms across her chest and paced in a tight circle. Suddenly her eyes flew open. "In the air."

"What?" Gadgets asked, rubbing his head.

"The toxin has to be released into the air. How many airplanes could be flying in this weather?"

HERBERT QUEENSBURY dusted the snow off his pants after removing the tarp from the stolen state trooper car. He could barely restrain himself from laughing. He had won. Now it was time for the losers to pay the price for failure. Queensbury pushed the button on the remote broadcast unit that would signal Potts it was time to drop the toxin.

The Gamesmaster started up the car and headed south. The winding mountain road was snow-covered and slick. A series of flares were set up along its sides to warn of the approaching roadblock. A local cop waved him through without even a cursory check.

"OLD BUDDY," the charter pilot said with a broad smile. "You may be crazy, but I'm not. There's no way I'm goin' up in this soup."

Brian Hall earned enough from May through October to live on for the entire year. For five bucks a head he would fly tourists on a scenic tour of the river valleys and the Summerville Dam's lake. On warm weekends, when the population of the area exploded with white water enthusiasts, he could easily clear two grand after expenses. This charter was just gravy.

"But we have a contract," Alfred Potts whined.

"I'll be happy to refund your deposit." The pilot took another sip from his cup of coffee. "But there's nothin' that'll get me to go up today."

"Oh, I don't know," Potts said.

In his right hand was a 9 mm Beretta automatic.

GADGETS WAS HUDDLED with Brognola. The head Fed was on an open line to the Oval Office. "You got it," Brognola barked to Gadgets. "Anything else?"

"A miracle."

"I've only got the President on the phone." Brognola's face was grim. "The best we can give you is a prayer."

"I'll take it," Gadgets answered. "Be sure someone picks up Ironman and Pol."

"Right. Good luck."

Gadgets nodded and headed toward the waiting helicopter. Grimaldi had the Sikorsky warmed up and ready to fly. They were in the air before Gadgets could get the sliding door closed.

"Where to?"

"The closest airport."

Metzger had anticipated the question and had already plotted the course. "The closest airstrip is just north of the Summerville Dam."

"An AWACS radar plane took off from Edwards Air Force Base," Gadgets explained. "He should have us under his radar umbrella in a few minutes."

"What, exactly, are we looking for?" Grimaldi asked.

"An airplane."

"Hey, Gadgets," Grimaldi said only seconds later after listening to a report that was coming in at the same time over his headphones, "the AWACS has picked up a light airplane. It just took off from the Summerville airport and appears to be headed east toward Washington."

"Where is it now?"

"Headed right at us."

"I've got it on radar," Metzger said. "Increase altitude to eight thousand feet and change your heading ten degrees to the east and we'll intersect her."

"Jack," Gadgets asked, "can you get close enough to make visual contact?"

"What kind of visual contact?"

"Close enough to see who's inside."

"If I had the stick—" Metzger shot a glance at Grimaldi "—I'd get you close enough to see the color of their eyes."

Grimaldi laughed. "Well, let's go see the color of their eyes."

In the cold weather, with the increased atmospheric density, the performance of the engines and the rotor of the Sikorsky improved. The big bird now handled like a chopper half its size.

The snow was falling steadily, which limited visibility. The winds had died down, but an occasional strong gust still buffeted the helicopter.

"We should be able to see them soon," Metzger announced. Gadgets leaned into the cockpit for a better view. "There," Metzger said, pointing at a red Beechcraft. "Eleven o'clock high."

"Got it," Grimaldi said as the helicopter increased speed and altitude. They closed the distance to less than two hundred yards.

"Will we be able to keep up with him?" Gadgets asked.

"Probably," Metzger answered. The Air Force captain radioed the twin-engine plane's call numbers back to the base, then tried to raise the plane by radio. "He's not responding."

"Maybe he doesn't see us," Gadgets offered.

"We'll take care of that." Grimaldi pulled back on the throttle, the nose of the chopper dipped, and they pulled up even with the Beechcraft.

Nan looked out the side window and shouted, "There's a man in the back with a gun pointed at the pilot." The airplane suddenly veered off to the left and dropped five hundred feet, and the Sikorsky followed.

HAL BROGNOLA WAS MONITORING the air chatter from the makeshift command center when he heard the second Sikorsky land. A minute later Lyons and Blancanales entered the room.

"What's up, boss?" Pol asked. "Why didn't Jack and Gadgets pick us up?"

"They may have a line on the toxin."

Ironman's eyes burned. "Where?"

"A plane took off a few minutes ago from an airport near here."

"Do they know if the toxin's on the plane?"

"Not yet." Brognola tossed his well-chewed cigar in the general direction of the wastebasket in the corner.

"We're going after them," Lyons announced.

"No, you're not," Brognola said firmly.

"Why not?" The rage inside of Carl Lyons threatened to push the tightly wound warrior over the edge if he didn't soon find a release. "I can't just sit here and do nothing."

"Yes, you can, Carl. You have to." Brognola unwrapped a fresh cigar and stuck it between his teeth. "What if the plane is just a businessman heading for a meeting? I can't afford to have both of these helicopters that far from here."

"Damn." Lyons slammed his fist into the wall. Normally the blow would have easily gone through the drywall, but Ironman's fist found one of the studs. Pol examined Lyons's hand. Nothing was broken, but the skin had been ripped from several of the knuckles.

"Real smart, Ironman," Pol said as he reached for a first-aid kit.

Lyons didn't answer, and if he noticed the pain in his hand, it didn't show. His eyes were focused a thousand miles away and his mind was working at the speed of light. Queensbury had beaten him. And millions of people were going to die.

BRIAN HALL REACHED for the microphone to answer the helicopter.

"Don't touch that," Potts said. He wiped his hand across the glass of the rear passenger window. He didn't like what he saw. The big Sikorsky was only a few hundred feet away. "Lose them," Potts ordered.

"You can't be serious," the pilot answered.

Potts jammed the barrel of his gun behind the pilot's right ear. "Do I look like I'm kidding?"

As the plane veered once again, Potts opened the two suitcases on the seat beside him.

"What's that stuff?" Hall asked, glancing over his shoulder.

"Just fly the plane." Potts's hands were shaking as he fumbled with the first container. The lid required two hands to open and Potts didn't want to lower his weapon. He wedged the container against the seat and tried again. The lid hissed as its airtight seal was broken.

METZGER PULLED DOWN the eyepiece of the roof-mounted sight for the Hellfire missile system. The laser guided antitank missile would make short work of the Beechcraft. "Get behind him, Jack."

"What are you doing?" Nan yelled.

"I'm about to blow up an airplane, ma'am," Metzger answered dryly.

"You can't!"

"Why not?" Gadgets asked.

"If the plane's blown up, the toxin will mix in midair. That's exactly what we're trying to avoid."

"She's got a point, Jack. We have to force the plane down. We can't blow it up."

Grimaldi scratched the back of his neck. "If we can't shoot at it, then I'm open to suggestions."

"I've got it," Metzger said. "Get as close to the rear of the plane as you can, but you have to be within five hundred meters."

"You're the boss, but why?"

"You wouldn't want one of these babies to blow up in your face. The Hellfire's warhead doesn't activate till it's traveled at least a thousand yards."

"I get it," Gadgets said. "Use it for a kinetic kill."

"Give the man a gold star."

"What are you talking about?" Nan demanded.

"We're going to throw a very expensive rock at our friend. Even without using the warhead, the missile will have enough mass and speed to blow a good-size hole in that plane."

A light clicked on in Nan's eyes. "And it will either have to land or it'll crash without blowing up in midair." Stein knitted her brow. "What if it hits the gas tank and blows up, anyway?"

Gadgets shrugged. "You got any better ideas?"

Stein didn't. She sat back, bracing herself for what was about to happen.

The Beechcraft tried everything possible to shake Grimaldi and the Sikorsky, but the Black Hawk was too fast and too maneuverable for the airplane.

"I've got a target lock," Metzger announced. "Nine hundred meters."

The nose of the Sikorsky dipped slightly as Grimaldi increased speed.

"Eight hundred meters. Seven hundred meters. Six hundred meters. Five hundred meters."

The passengers in the Black Hawk felt the vibration and heard a rumble from the left side launch ramp. A moment later they saw the red tail of the Hellfire as it roared toward its target.

"Missile away." Metzger held the laser on the center of the Beechcraft. The glass-nosed Hellfire slammed into the tail section, passed through the fiberglass body of the plane and continued on course. At one thousand meters, with the impact switch already activated, the safety was released. The Hellfire erupted like a Fourth of July fireworks show.

The Beechcraft was losing altitude. The forty-five-kilogram rocket had sheared all of the control cables, and aviation fuel streamed from a ruptured fuel tank. First one engine and then the other sputtered and stopped. The crippled Beechcraft plowed nose first into the West Virginia mountains.

EPILOGUE

Nan Stein's foot slipped in the snow, and Gadgets helped her to her feet. The self-contained units they were wearing were designed for handling toxic waste, not for mountain climbing. Borrowed from the EPA in Washington, the white outfits looked like something out of the space program. Completely sealed inside the awkward outfit, with air provided from tanks carried on the back, they had found the trip to the crash sight a formidable task.

"Are these things really necessary?" Gadgets asked into the built-in microphone.

"Only if the containers have been breached," Nan answered. Gadgets could see her smile through the fogged glass of the headgear. "We'll know in a few minutes."

On impact the Beechcraft had broken into three pieces but hadn't burned. Fearing that the rotor of the helicopter might stir any spilled toxin into the atmosphere, they had decided to walk nearly half a mile to the crash site. Six men from the EPA Hazardous Waste Division had accompanied them.

Fifty feet from the wreckage the decapitated body of the pilot was draped over a low-hanging tree branch. The missing head was wedged between two branches twenty feet higher in the tree. Alfred Potts had somehow managed to survive the crash and was still strapped to the rear seat of the Beechcraft. The seat had ripped away from the plane and was thirty yards from the bulk of the wreckage.

Before impact Potts had managed to get the lid off the second container of the toxin. The two parts had combined with the moisture of the snow to form a deadly brew. Potts's swollen tongue protruded from his mouth, and his face showed the strain of trying to breathe through his closed throat.

"Damn!" one of the EPA men muttered.

IT HAD TAKEN Aaron Kurtzman three days to track down the bug that Queensbury had planted in the Stony Man computer system. "Brilliant," Bear said to himself.

"What's brilliant?" Brognola asked as he made his way through the mass of printouts scattered from one end of the room to the other.

"Hey, boss." Kurtzman underlined a section of one of the printouts with a highlighter. "Queensbury's bug was absolutely brilliant. It was next to impossible to find because he shut down the monitors. I had to make hard copies of everything and go over the programs line by line."

"You got it fixed?"

"I'll tell you in a second." Kurtzman pivoted in his chair and stroked the keyboard. One by one his monitors clicked back to life. "It wasn't even that sophisticated a virus, but turning off the CRTs was a masterstroke."

"How bad was the security leak?"

Kurtzman sighed. "Hard to say. I run all of the Stony Man information through my own code, which I doubt even Queensbury could crack. Most of the info he intercepted that wasn't encoded was classified but not sensitive."

"No damage done?" Brognola asked hopefully.

"I don't think so. I'll go back over the information and get back to you."

"I'd appreciate it."

"Where are the guys?"

"Pol and Carl are over in the gym, and Gadgets and Dr. Stein decided to take a week off in the Bahamas."

"The cleanup work's all finished?"

"Yeah," Brognola answered. "And all of the toxin's accounted for. The part that spilled has been neutralized and the rest is back in Iowa. We were lucky that it wasn't mixed into the clouds."

"How's Ironman?"

Brognola shook his head. "I've never seen him like this before. When he heard the police had let Queensbury slip through the roadblocks, he went crazy."

"I heard he punched somebody," Bear said, smiling.

"Somebody! That's a laugh. He decked the chief of the West Virginia State Police. If the President hadn't stepped in, Carl would be in jail right now."

"Still no line on Queensbury?"

Brognola unwrapped a cigar and looked for a place to throw the cellophane. With the mess in the computer room, he just dropped it on the floor. "It's as if he never existed."

CARL LYONS GRUNTED with every punch. Pol did his best to steady the heavy bag, but each blow made him take a step back. The front of Ironman's shirt was dark with perspiration, and his blond hair was matted to his scalp.

"Let's take a break, amigo," Pol suggested.

"I'm not tired." Ironman's eyes burned as he continued his assault on the punching bag.

"You may not be tired, but I am." Pol let go of the bag, and the last punch by Ironman almost sent it to the gym floor. It swayed back and forth on the chain connected to a stud in the ceiling.

One of the Stony Man guards stuck his head in the door of the gym and located Lyons. "Hey, Ironman, come out here. Quick!"

Lyons dropped the towel he was using to wipe his face and sprinted toward the door. Outside, a model plane was buzzing the complex. Ironman snatched the M-16 out of the startled guard's hands and opened fire. The plane spun to the ground near the motor pool. Lyons dropped the smoking weapon and sprinted toward the model. Taped to the wing of the airplane was a letter addressed to one Carl Lyons. He ripped the envelope open and read the note. All of the color drained from his face.

Lyons's gunfire had caused all of the buildings at Stony Man to empty. Ironman, surrounded by his friends and co-workers, dropped the note into the snow and headed back to the gym. Pol picked up the piece of paper and read it out loud.

You put me in prison, but I got free.
You got the toxin, but you couldn't catch me.
So now we're tied, you have to agree.
What say we go for the best two out of three?

A breakaway faction of NATO plots to "free" Europe from the superpowers.

THE BARRABAS SWEEP

JACK HILD

The Realm, a murderous faction of NATO powered by a covert network of intelligence, paramilitary and corporate empires across Europe, proposes to liberate the continent from NATO. It's an infallible plan designed for destruction — until ex-Special Forces colonel Nile Barrabas and his crack commando squad step in.

Do you know a real hero?

At Gold Eagle Books we know that heroes are not just fictional. Everyday someone somewhere is performing a selfless task, risking his or her own life without expectation of reward.

Gold Eagle would like to recognize America's local heroes by publishing their stories. If you know a true to life hero (that person might even be you) we'd like to hear about him or her. In 150-200 words tell us about a heroic deed you witnessed or experienced. Once a month, we'll select a local hero and award him or her with national recognition by printing his or her story on the inside back cover of THE EXECUTIONER series, and the ABLE TEAM, PHOENIX FORCE and/or VIETNAM: GROUND ZERO series.

Send your name, address, zip or postal code, along with your story of 150-200 words (and a photograph of the hero if possible), and mail to:

LOCAL HEROES AWARD
Gold Eagle Books
225 Duncan Mill Road
Don Mills, Ontario
M3B 3K9
Canada